Probably Still Nick Swansen

VIRGINIA EUWER WOLFF

SIMON PULSE
New York London Toronto Sydney Singapore

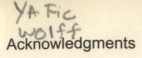

Acknowledgments

Mary Cash, Marilyn E. Marlow, Eugene Euwer,
Nicholas A. Wheeler, Michael Fitzgerald, and
Christina Anderson aided in the progress of this story.

First Simon Pulse edition October 2002

SIMON PULSE
An imprint of Simon & Schuster
Children's Publishing Division
1230 Avenue of the Americas
New York, NY 10020

Designed by Ann Sullivan
The text of this book was set in Bembo.

Printed and bound in the United States of America
10 9 8 7 6 5 4

The Library of Congress has cataloged the hardcover edition as follows:
Wolff, Virginia Euwer.
Probably Still Nick Swansen / by Virginia Euwer Wolff.
Summary: Sixteen-year-old learning-disabled Nick struggles to endure a life in which the other kids make fun of him, he has to take special classes, his date for the prom makes an excuse not to go with him, and he is haunted by the memory of his older sister, who drowned while he was watching.
ISBN 0-8050-0701-6 (hc.)
[1. Learning disabilities—Fiction. 2. Self-acceptance—Fiction. 3. Death—Fiction. 4. Brothers and sisters—Fiction.] I. Title.
PZ7.W82129Pr 1988
[Fic]—dc19 88-13175

ISBN 0-689-85226-6 (Simon Pulse pbk.)

*for Anthony and Juliet
again*

Author's Note

This book contains some incorrect grammar and punctuation in order to tell Nick Swansen's story in language that is consistent with his.

April 30, 1988

. . . In yourself you labor, you wage and combat, settle scores, remember insults, fight, reply, deny, blab, denounce, triumph, outwit, overcome, vindicate, cry, persist, absolve, die and rise again. All by yourself! Where is everybody? Inside your breast and skin, the entire cast.

—Saul Bellow, *The Adventures of Augie March*

1

Room 19 was dressed up. It crackled with sounds, and party smells came from everywhere. Green streamers hung off the ceiling, two tables were covered with junk food, and more things were arriving every time you turned around—hot dogs, homemade brownies, three kinds of potato chips. A giant homemade poster was trying to come unhinged from its masking tape over the blackboard, and it said in huge red letters, "Yay Shana."

Shana had watched the decorating, but now two girls were keeping her in the bathroom while the final things got done. Bruce was twisting into his cheerleading skirt and sweater for the skit, and people were checking out places to hide when the warning came, so they could all jump up at once and yell Surprise.

Nick Swansen pushed a fallen potato chip back onto its plate, tied his left sneaker, which didn't need tying, got his elbow poked by a girl rushing in with ice cubes for the punch, and didn't poke her back. He watched the last-minute kids signing Shana's enormous balloon in thick magic markers, holding the markers lightly so they wouldn't break the balloon to pieces, and he stood near a window, looking.

The Going Up party had traditions, Nick had been watching them since he was fourteen, three years. Because he was fourteen then and sixteen now. It had to be a surprise, and it had to have food, decorations, and a program. It had to have a souvenir for the person. And this party was always for somebody who would stop being Special Ed. the next day and start being just like everybody else.

Today's food was the usual, but with a cake that Jill and some other kids had baked in the home ec. room. The decorations were the usual, but this time they were mostly green, probably for St. Patrick's Day coming, and for good luck.

Not that one color was any more good luck than any other color. Colors could be terrible luck, too.

Today's program would be Bruce doing his Shelley Cheerleader skit. Bruce had all kinds of trouble remembering things in school, but he was the funniest person in Room 19, so Mr. Norton said he should make up a comedy skit and do it by memory. Nick had seen part of it last week, he did a favor to Bruce watching and telling which was a good part.

The souvenir had to be something the person could carry home. Sometimes it was ridiculous, like the time they gave David Bertram the old smelly sneaker with a red ribbon around it and it was filled with carrots, candy bars, and pickles, and it had his first grade picture on it. That was last year. David stopped coming back to say hello a long time ago. He probably didn't even know about Shana's party today.

Shana's souvenir was much better. The green balloon was so big they could hardly get it through the door, and it had everybody's name on it, the way you sign somebody's cast for a broken leg. And it had silk flowers attached, purple and yellow and blue and pink and red, tied about eight inches apart all down the string.

But Shana wasn't supposed to see it yet. She knew she'd get a souvenir, but she wasn't supposed to know what it was until the class got ready to give it to her.

And she didn't know. When the girls brought her from the bathroom, you could tell she didn't have any idea there would be a green balloon that was bigger than she was. She just let the girls bring her into the room, she even looked calm, but you could tell she was just trying to look that way.

She had this really expecting look, in her chin and in her eyebrows. It was a look you might get on your face in front of a waterfall if you didn't know how far it might be falling before you saw it.

Nick liked Shana's face, God or somebody put it together in a happy way, she was nice when she smiled, and she smiled a lot.

Yelling Surprise along with everybody else was fun this time, even though it was a little-kid thing to do. The whole party was a little-kid thing, but they did it because it was a tradition. Shana looked surprised at all the food and things, and you could tell she liked it. She still didn't know about the balloon.

Bruce got in front of the class with the pom-poms, all

3

blue and gold and white, and he was Shelley Cheerleader, and she couldn't remember the name of the team. "Let's all give a cheer for the Bears—I mean the Tigers—I mean the Eagles. . . ." Then she forgot the arm motions, and then she forgot the dance steps, and she stood there waving her pom-poms.

The next part of his skit was the team scores. Bruce pretended Shelley Cheerleader couldn't remember any of them.

Then came the strip-act. Bruce used a tape recorder for this part, he said he couldn't strip without music. He had a tape of the school band. He took off the sweater, and the skirt, and then his T-shirt, and then his pants, with the fight song playing, and he still had on high-topped sneakers and swimming trunks, and then he sort of danced over to the aquarium that Room 19 kept with the swordfish and the bleeding heart tetras and some others, and he pretended to dive into the water. That was the end of the skit.

Everybody clapped, and some people yelled, "Hey, Skateboard!" Skateboard was Bruce's other name, from his project last year.

Then it was time to eat. The giant balloon was still hidden in the closet, and everybody except Shana would know what the terrible pop was if a ruler or something in the closet stuck into the balloon. Nick thought about Eeyore's birthday party.

Sometimes he thought he was terribly weird to worry so much about that party, it was only a little-kids' story. Winnie-the-Pooh tried to take a jar of honey to Eeyore for his birthday, but he couldn't help eating all the honey on his way through the forest to Eeyore's Gloomy Place. And Piglet had a balloon for Eeyore, left over from his own birthday. On his way through the forest, Piglet fell down on top of the balloon and broke it. It used to be a red balloon before it broke.

You thought the sad part was going to be about getting the empty present and the broken present, but you were wrong. The sad part was when Eeyore put the broken balloon in the empty jar and then he took it out, and then he put it in and he took it out again. And that was the way he celebrated his birthday. Nick's mother had put her arm around him because he cried when she read that part to him. She said, "Isn't it nice that poor Eeyore can be happy after all?" Nick was wearing Snoopy pajamas then, and his sister was still alive.

Nick would like his sister now. Even back then, when she was ten, she could play songs on her recorder, "Oh! Susannah" and "Twinkle Twinkle." They slept together sometimes, on cold nights, underneath the sleeping bag filled with goose feathers, even when they weren't camping. Dianne had long reddish braids and green shorts. Everybody in the family had sleeping bags, and Mom and Dad had ones that zipped together when they went camping, but then they were called Mommy and Daddy.

"I'm the only man who has a sleeping bag that zips together with yours," his dad said, and Nick smelled the trout cooking in the pan on the camp fire. Dianne was a good fish catcher, and Nick went along in the boat.

"And I'm the only lady with a sleeping bag that zips together with yours," his mother laughed.

Dianne asked them once, What about the other people that bought their sleeping bags at the Mountain Shop? Couldn't they zip theirs together with either Daddy's or

Mommy's, if they had the right kind of zipper and they put it together with our family's zippers?

Mommy and Daddy laughed and Daddy said, "Those guys are all camping at another lake." Mommy worked at the fish in the pan with a fork.

Dianne wondered how that could be, and she asked them: How could all those other people be at another lake?

Daddy laughed again, and said something like "They're all looking for your mommy because she's the prettiest lady at any of the lakes, but I won her, I've got the only matching bag."

Dianne had to have it explained, about winning Mommy. It was good to have Dianne around then, she could ask the questions when Nick couldn't think of the words. He didn't know about winning Mommy either, like winning a smiley face from the teacher if you colored in the lines. But Dianne knew just how to ask. "How did you win Mommy? Did you do a contest?"

They ate the fish on clinking metal plates, and they had garlic bread with the fish. Daddy cooked the garlic bread in silver foil in the coals, in the special garlic-bread zone of the coals, he knew how to find the zone. Nick didn't know until a long time later that there wasn't a real garlic-bread zone, Daddy just named it that out of his head. Dianne never found that out.

Nick stood, stirring what was left of the potato salad without having any reason to stir it, watching Shana and the Room 19 kids playing Movie Titles, and thinking about the sleeping bags that zipped together, and the way Dad and Mom, when they were Daddy and Mommy, told about winning Mommy. It wasn't a real contest.

"The first time I noticed your mommy was when she argued with our history teacher in college. She was the only person in the class to argue with him. And I looked at her, sitting in her chair with this proud look on her face, and I talked to her on the way out of the room."

"He told me I had pretty teeth. What a weird way to get to know a girl."

Dianne laughed every time they told it. She said, "He was a *den*tist, Mommy!"

"Darling, I didn't know that then—I just thought—"

"And I wasn't a dentist, I was just *going* to be a dentist—"

"Did you help the poor men and ladies then?" Dianne asked Mommy. She liked to know when things happened. It was just something she liked to know, if something happened before or after something else.

"No, love. I was still in school, and we didn't even live in Portland. I don't think Free Lunch was even started yet."

Mommy used to take Nick and Dianne with her to Free Lunch sometimes, and she let them give out the spoons and paper napkins to the people who ate their food there. Free Lunch always smelled like spaghetti but there was other food too, and you could watch the jello jiggling when the people carried it on their plates. Once Nick and Dianne got to help make a big cake, it covered a whole table. It was for a birthday and the old man in the wheel-chair blew out the candles, there were eight candles but Mommy told them he was more than eight years old.

"Did you have your blessings back then? When Daddy told you about your teeth?" Dianne asked.

Mommy laughed. "Sure, honey. I just didn't have as many." Then she started her list. "A goose down sleeping bag that zips into Daddy's, and two excellent, wonderful children, and pieces of trout between my teeth, and a piano with only 106 payments left to make, and little old men who stop me on the street to tell me Daddy's the best dentist in the world—"

"About your blessings of me!" Dianne said.

"I said two excellent, wonderful children—"

"But about your girl child." Dianne always wanted to hear about those blessings again. Smoke from the camp fire puffed up in front of her.

"A fine, strong girl child. She has the best red braids in the country, she practices her recorder every day, she catches small trout—"

"This is a big one, Daddy said it was a big one for me to catch!"

"Right, sweetheart. She catches big trout. Oh yes: and she does forty-one trampoline bounces without stopping. . . ."

"And she can swim!" Dianne almost shouted through the smoke. Somebody was saying, "Hey, Skateboard, take a swim!" It was Alex; he meant in the aquarium with the swordfish. Because Bruce still had swimming trunks on.

Mr. Norton got his camera out of his pack. He liked to take pictures of Going Up parties. "This one's gonna be great, sports fans. Bruce, put on the whole outfit again. The sweater and skirt, don't forget the pom-poms. We're gonna go outside for this picture. Color by Room 19."

There were the usual moans, from people who never wanted their pictures taken, and then some noise about blindfolding Shana and leading her outside by the hand.

Shana said, "I'm game. You're not gonna put my hand in something awful, are you?"

8

More laughter. "No, we're just giving you a real Going Up," said one of the girls.

Somebody had a sweater, lying across a chair, and they used it to blindfold her. Next, hand signals went across the room for somebody to open the closet door and get her souvenir balloon out. Nick was closest to the closet, so it was his job.

It was the last period of the day, and most people were still in class, so they had to be quiet going outside. Three girls led Shana, two holding her hands and one nudging her. Everyone tried to be quiet, but Bruce in his cheer-leading costume was too much, and several people, Mr. Norton included, couldn't help laughing.

Nick carried the balloon, worrying that it might get caught on something, and Eeyore and his birthday came into his mind again. The sun was shining, just enough to make you squint. Two people turned cartwheels on the grass, you could always count on some people to do that the minute everyone got outside, even if they never did it any other time.

March could be dry and sunny in Oregon, or it could be rainy. The Oregon jokes about rain all the time weren't true, but people laughed at them anyway.

Becky grabbed the balloon string from Nick. She whispered, "It's my turn now—the balloon was my idea," and Nick let go of the string.

Jill took the sweater off Shana's eyes. Becky stood in front of her, holding the balloon with its silk flowers down the string, and the signed names revolved in the air, the sun making them blurry.

"Yowee! It's great!" Shana blinked, and shielded her

eyes with one hand while she reached for the string with the other. She liked it, she was so pretty when she smiled, and she didn't even have popcorn or potato chip pieces stuck to her clothes. "You guys, I'm always gonna remember you!" She looked at the flowers, moving her hands up the string until they rested between the purple flower and the yellow one.

"Everybody move in closer. Bunch up. Shana, where do you want to stand?" Mr. Norton lifted the camera to his eyes, lowered it, and lifted it again, as if he was practicing.

Shana held her big balloon and looked around her. Her eyes were still having trouble getting used to the sunlight. Even blinking and staring around, she was so pretty.

Nick didn't know why Shana moved in next to him in the group. She had sixteen people to choose from. He moved over to make room for her. The green balloon floated above them; he looked up at it and watched it swirl in the sun.

"Hey, come on over here and stand by me," Jason Bartholomew said, with his fingertips in the sides of his mouth, making a terrible face. Becky and Jill looked at each other, and Jill shrugged her shoulders.

Nick felt strange: Why should you get excited because somebody stands next to you in a picture? And why would Shana want to stand by me? And what's a picture, anyway? Just somebody's idea of a good time, to put on the bulletin board later.

"Come on, troops, move in closer—this is a camera I bought with my teacher's salary!" Nick was bumped from the right and from the front as people moved in, some of them in Bugs Bunny positions.

10

"I wish he'd get this over with," Nick muttered. He knew he was muttering, but he had to say something. Shana was standing right there next to him, the balloon making a shadow over his face.

Shana was pulling it down by the string, her hands going over each silk flower. "I want to find your name, Nick. Where is it?"

He couldn't remember. Next to Jason's, maybe, or next to Becky's. "I don't know," he said.

"Here it is." Shana had the balloon in front of both their faces now, steadying it with one arm, reading. "Nick, that's hysterical—'Where is Up?' What a great thing to write. I'm gonna remember that one." She laughed and laughed, and let the balloon go to the length of the string.

He'd been thinking of David Bertram, the one you never saw anymore. He'd just written Where is Up? That was all. Nothing to get excited about.

Shana was whispering in his left ear. "You're the most mature person in this whole class."

He looked at her. He shrugged his shoulders and just looked at her. He wished he knew a way to look, but he didn't.

He wasn't mature. He wasn't anything, just somebody alive, that was all.

"Jason and Alex, will you cut it out?" Mr. Norton's voice was still trying to make itself heard.

Shana leaned her head on Nick's shoulder, the hand right next to him clutching the balloon string between the purple and yellow flowers. The string was almost between his eyes. She whispered again, and he leaned down to hear her. "You be sure to invite me to your Going Up."

She had to be kidding. "You're kidding," he whispered back.

"I'm not. You'll be next."

"I won't." Now he turned to face her sideways, looking down at her nose. Boy, it was a pretty nose.

"Yes, I'm not kidding. You'll be next. Just keep morking."

Without knowing he was going to laugh, Nick laughed. He'd miss Shana. She remembered morking. He thought he was the only one.

She changed the balloon string to her left hand and took hold of Nick's hand with her right one. There was a bright sky and she was holding his hand and it was the last period of the day and it was a party in March in Portland and there was no rain, and nobody else in the world knew why they were laughing, and the balloon swung over their two heads, moving its shadow, and her hand felt joyful and fine in his hand, and he and she both remembered morking hard and nobody else would ever figure it out and the camera clicked with Nick's mouth wide open, as if he was eating sunshine.

"Hold still, ladies and gentlemen, let's make sure we've got a good one in this batch," Mr. Norton said, and everyone managed to hold partly still for about four more shots.

If Nick had been born Bruce, he'd know how to be funny back when Shana said that, but he wasn't Bruce. Instead, while he was laughing about morking, he tried to remember, for later, just how Shana looked when she said it, talking to his neck. Her skirt had puffed out a little, she'd probably bent her knees; and her elbow, on the arm she was holding his hand with, poked his ribs just above his belt.

Her voice sounded almost like a secret voice, one she might not use with other people except maybe Jill and Becky. But maybe he was wrong: Her voice was secret, but maybe not that much secret. Her head, for sure, shook a little bit. And it shook a little bit more when Nick laughed.

He had to say something back, you had to say something, you couldn't just laugh. You had to let her know you heard what she said.

"Yeah, I'll mork hard," he said. Shana smiled at the camera and let go of his hand.

The rest of the pictures got taken and the party broke up.

Nick never told anybody about morking.

Last year, there was a kid who wasn't in Room 19 very long because he got caught stealing things from a store and got sent away from his foster home. They had one of the quizzes that Mr. Norton loved to give just after lunch. What is your favorite color, and why? Who is the vice-president of the United States? What is or was your mother's middle name or her maiden name? What is the worst thing about this school, and why? What is the first thing you do when you go home from school? Tell us one thing you've learned today. What should we do to make Room 19's walls more attractive? Name something you've never done. Why have you never done it? Tell us one funny thing that has happened this week.

The two Down's syndrome kids were the only ones who didn't have to answer all the questions, and they didn't have to write their answers, they could say them to Mr. Norton. They only came to Room 19 sometimes, anyway. Other days they went someplace else. Everybody else had to take the whole quiz. The quizzes got graded, and your grade depended on how careful you were in thinking of the answers. Spelling didn't count. Most of the people in Room 19 were used to the quizzes, but not this new kid.

This kid, and Nick had forgotten his name, wrote on the top of his quiz, "Please don't flunk me, I morked hard."

Shana saw it when she turned in her paper, and she was sitting next to Nick that day, and when she came back to her chair she told him.

A few days later, the new kid disappeared, they never heard about him again except he was a shoplifter. Nick knew, as he was going home on the day of Shana's party, that he should have asked her what that new kid's name was.

Now, at home after the party, Nick hugged his dog Patsy and started really thinking about Dianne.

Would she cut her braids off when she went to high school? You never knew, but her braids might still be there, long and reddish. She had freckles, and by now she'd have breasts. Nick added in his head, and knew she'd be nineteen this year.

Two things were important now: one, don't think about Dianne because of the bad dream, and two, now is the time to have a sister to talk to.

Dianne was regular, she didn't have Special Ed. She'd know the answers he needed now, of course.

Hey, Dianne, he'd knock on the door of her room, except they'd moved from that house. She didn't have a room here. Hey, Dianne, he knocked on her imaginary door, to the room she didn't have. How do you know if a girl likes you?

He sat in his room, his elbows on the desk he and his father built together. It was a good desk, solid in the corners, and the drawers all fit. Patsy sat watching him with her head on his knee.

What if a girl reaches down during a photograph and holds your hand? Does she like you?

Dianne let Mommy braid her hair and then she jumped on the trampoline. Was it really forty-one jumps without stopping? What a strong little kid.

Dianne, you're so smart, what if you and this girl have a joke together and you're positive nobody else knows? Does she like you then? He ran his hand down the desk leg clear to the floor. Are there some guys that girls never like? Listen, Dianne. You know. Tell me.

A siren ran by, a few blocks away. Somebody's house was on fire. Don't you know I have to find out the answers? Cut out that awful noise.

Dianne smiled in the photograph on his desk, from her tenth birthday party, with five other girls, everyone wearing dresses.

Listen, Dianne. Is there some way you could know if a girl likes you?

No answer.

That was the way it would always be with Dianne. Smiling, being a little girl he used to think was so big, and she'd never say anything to him now.

When Nick took off his sweater that night, he found a longish, dark-blondish, bendy hair on the left shoulder of it. Oh boy, he thought. Shana left her hair on my sweater and she doesn't even know it. He put it on his desk and put a ruler on one end of it so it wouldn't drift away.

Now he really needed to know if she liked him, but there was nobody to ask. Jason Bartholomew was okay, but you couldn't ask him that question. Bruce, too: You couldn't ask him anything like that.

2

Two times in the next week Shana came back to Room 19 to say hello, but once was during lunch and she just left a note on the blackboard: Hello—Shana. And she drew a picture of a big balloon with sort of flowers on its string.

She wasn't even around for April Fool's Day, when somebody filled Mr. Norton's desk drawers with potato chips. She might not think it was very funny, anyway.

Her locker was eight lockers away from Nick's, and they saw each other sometimes in the mornings, not every morning. And some afternoons. It was hard, not knowing what to say except, Hi, how're ya doing? That was something you could say to just anybody, and they always knew you didn't even listen to the answer.

One morning Nick walked right over to her and asked her if she was morking hard. She laughed her pretty laugh and rolled her eyes. "You don't have any idea how hard! Keep the faith, baby!" And she ran off to class.

By late April, Nick had tried several more times to talk

with Dianne. Same thing. No answer. His dog Patsy watched him as he sat at his desk asking questions. Man's best friend: Patsy would never go and tell anybody how crazy he was for trying to talk to somebody dead.

The prom was coming, and Nick was thinking about it. He couldn't remember any Room 19 kids going to a prom, but somebody might have. Why couldn't you just up and go to the prom? Why couldn't he just go to the prom with Shana? No rule said you couldn't. It began as a sort of thought in his head one day, and pretty soon it was a bigger thought, because he made a list of things he'd have to do. Mr. Norton was big on lists. He said they help you get organized, they help you understand what you're thinking. Nick sat on his bedroom floor and wrote the list. Learn to dance, rent a tuxedo, earn money to buy the tickets. Buy a corsage to go with the color of the dress the girl would wear, figure out how to get to the prom. Lots of things wouldn't even fit on the paper. He put it in the bottom drawer of his desk where nobody would see it.

Shana was always flying off to her other classes, and she had so many new girlfriends it looked like a boatload every time she stopped at her locker.

"Hi, Nick, morking hard?" was just about all she said to him now. But at least it wasn't just, Hi, how're ya doing?

And she had held his hand.

He kept looking at the wildlife calendar on his bedroom wall. The picture for May was of two honeybees on apple blossoms. He started to make a count of the days in his mind: twenty-six, twenty-five, twenty-four, going backward to the day of the prom, day zero.

When the count was at twenty, Nick decided to do what

he maybe shouldn't do. He might be really sorry, but there was nobody to talk to about it, so he brushed his teeth very hard, practiced saying it to the bathroom mirror nearly twenty times, and then walked to school early and hung around his locker until he could say it really. It was Monday.

"Hi, Shana. You want to go to the prom?" It came out faster than he thought it would. Suddenly he thought he needed a haircut. And he suddenly hated the braces on his teeth. He wished he wasn't so skinny.

"Hi, Nick. You're kidding."

He had to say something. "No. You want to go to the prom?" He should have been a football player, or at least baseball.

She stood next to her locker, with one foot propped on the edge of it, balancing a load of books in her arms. Her face was joking, he thought. But then she said, "Sure. Really? Are you asking me to the prom?"

Suddenly he had all kinds of guts. "Sure. You want to go with me?" So that's how they ask girls to proms, he discovered. They just do it. It just comes out of their mouths. He almost laughed.

"Gee." She made a face. "I've got these tests this week." She squinted and shrugged at the same time. "But yeah. Yeah, sure. I want to go."

"You really do?"

"I really do."

And she was off to her first period class, and now Nick was going to the prom. He walked down the hall with his books, saying words in his mind. Corsage. Tuxedo. Long dress. What color? Dancing. Music. Pretty Shana. Money. The prom.

Of course his parents would drive him to the prom, at a fancy hotel ballroom on the bank of the Columbia River. Of course they'd help with the money if he couldn't earn it all himself, but—

And he would work extra hours in the greenhouse to pay for the flowers and the—no problem.

And of course he would learn to dance.

Beginning that morning, day twenty, Bruce in Room 19 wasn't very funny anymore, and Nick got tired of talking to Jason Bartholomew. He still had to do his year-end project, but that was amphibians, no problem.

And on the night of day twenty, he began to learn to dance. He scattered books and shoes and underwear across the floor in his bedroom, like an obstacle course, and played music on the radio. You had to watch the people dancing on TV, and then you had to do it by memory. Dianne couldn't help, and he practiced by himself, watching his feet in the mirror on his bedroom door. He had to make up a rule for Patsy: If she'd lie down on his bed, she could stay in the room while he practiced, but if she got excited he'd send her out. The rule was No Dog Dancing. Because she took up too much space and you could trip over her.

On day sixteen, when his mother had dropped him off early at school, Shana was at her locker without the crowd of girls. Nick asked her the question he'd wanted to ask her for a long time.

"Hi, Shana. What're you gonna wear to the prom?" It came out so smoothly, now that there was no problem about going to the prom.

"Hi. Algebra's terrible, don't ever take it. What?"

"What's your dress, for the prom, the color?" He felt his

voice fading out. If he hadn't had to ask her twice . . .

"Oh, that. It's lavender, and it has flowers on it—if my mother and I ever finish making it. The darned sewing machine had to go for repairs—you know . . ."

"Oh, that's great, that's. . . ."

"What?" Shana had her head in her locker, looking for something.

He felt silly. "I said lavender's just great!"

She pulled her head out into the air. "You don't have to *yell* at me, Nicholas," she said. She slammed her locker door shut and walked off.

On day fifteen, Nick went to the florist and asked for a wrist corsage of pink flowers. He knew from the greenhouse what flowers would keep for a day or two after the dance. Small pink rosebuds would go leathery but they wouldn't fall apart.

Shana was really going to the prom, she was really his date. The dancing practice was getting easier, because he did it every night.

On day thirteen he told her he didn't mean to yell at her and she said it was okay.

He asked about the sewing machine repairs and the dress, and she lifted her head up sideways and laughed twice at the ceiling of the hallway before she said, "Don't *worry*." It was kind of a shadowy way that girls sometimes talked when they had a bunch of books in their arms.

By day ten, Nick had enough money for the prom tickets. The committee girl who sold the tickets knew he was going to the prom with Shana. The whole world seemed to know. "We're putting up balloons with all the names on them. What color's Shana's dress?" she wanted to know.

21

"It's lavender," he told her. He thought there might be people who would just stand there and not know what color to say. The girl said lavender was a terrific color, but she didn't have to say that: Nick knew.

She was taking his twenty dollars and giving him two tickets and saying, "Sure—we've got lavender balloons" to somebody else. "You going on the boat ride after?" she asked Nick.

Boat ride.

"You know, the *boat* ride. Up the Columbia to see the sun rise. Breakfast on board. And chaperons."

Nick had spent seven hours extra in the greenhouse to earn the money for the prom tickets, and his parents had volunteered to pay for the tuxedo rental, and he was working three hours this week for the corsage. "How much extra?" he said.

"Nine each, eighteen for the boat ride. You want tickets?"

"Take his I.O.U. Nick, give her your I.O.U." The varsity shortstop had his arm around Nick's shoulders. They try to pretend everybody's the same, but everybody's not, and a varsity arm around you isn't just an arm, and everybody knows it. This guy never even talked to Nick before.

Words came slipping out. "No problem," said Nick, and he signed his name on the official prom I.O.U.

"You've gotta pay by next Friday," the committee girl said cheerfully, and Nick walked off with his tickets.

Shana liked the idea of the boat ride. Standing by her locker door on the afternoon of day ten, Nick knew she didn't know how many hours he'd be watering plants and transplanting seedlings and repotting big tough things that had begun to curl their roots around and around the insides of pots that were too small.

He was embarrassed by how dirty his fingernails were when he bent over, right in front of Shana, to pick up a wrinkled scrap of paper that dropped out of her notebook. While he was standing up to give it to her, he read it fast.

YOUR NOT IN HIS CLASS ANYMORE ANYWAY

That was a really disturbing thing, Nick decided. Somebody in Shana's class maybe thought she was a little bit weird to go to the prom with somebody in Room 19. But Shana smiled and thanked him for picking it up and she stuffed it in her purse, so there was no problem, probably.

He went back to the greenhouse after school for his two hours of work, and thought about "probably," about how it kept coming up all the time. Probably he'd pass the Tuesday science quiz, but you never knew; probably his mother would cook a good dinner, but you never knew. Probably was every single thing, and it was all the time, and it could really (probably) make you crazy if you worried too much about it.

It had its good side: Probably the bomb wouldn't drop tomorrow, the way it dropped on Mr. Wakamatsu's family in Japan; probably Shana would hold his hand after dancing, probably his project of amphibians would be okay, probably everything would be all right for a while.

On day five, Mr. Norton said to Nick, before anybody else had gotten to class yet, "So. You and Shana are going to the prom?"

"Yeah." Nick wasn't sure he wanted Mr. Norton to know.

"Well, good for you. That's terrific."

"What do you mean?"

"I mean good for you, that's terrific. That's all."

He looked at Mr. Norton. Everybody had a first date sometime. Mr. Norton had one, for sure. The things Nick wanted to know were stuff nobody would probably tell him. He wanted to ask some things. But then, what were those things?

He tried very hard to decide what the questions were, and he couldn't find them. What do you? How do you? What do you do when, how do you do what? What did he mean? What do you mean, Nick—what do you do when and how do you do what? What do you mean, Nick? Inside his brain was a terrible asking voice, almost yelling at him: What do you *mean*?

If he asked anybody, that's what he'd hear, for sure. What do you *mean*, Nick?

You never could just say, I don't understand. You had to say *what* you didn't understand. But how could you tell somebody what it was if you didn't know what it was?

How do you not have bad breath at the prom? Easy: brush your teeth a lot before you go. That wasn't the problem. It was bigger things. He kicked a chair and it moved about three feet across Room 19.

The door opened and in came some kids, laughing and trying to trip each other.

Mr. Norton was suddenly talking softly in his ear. "You worried about stepping on her feet dancing, Nick? Everybody does it. You just say excuse me and laugh, then she says excuse me and she laughs. Nothing to it. Trust me." And he walked away.

That wasn't it. Not really. Well, wait a minute. That was a little bit of it. But Mr. Norton was old. Thirty-two, they had his party in the winter. Maybe that's the way they did it in the old days.

Nick sat down and got ready for school to start.

If he wasn't Special Ed., he'd know what to do, and he'd know how to do it. He looked at the awful, smiling poster on the wall of Room 19, the one with kids grinning at their desks. "I'm Special, and I get a Special Education in America." And in little tiny print at the bottom, "Public Law 94–142 means *you*." Nick had a terrible thought: I could pick my nose and wipe my finger straight across the whole poster, sometime when my dad and I've been working with the wood and sawdust and my nose is full of awful junk. Nobody would know if I did it when nobody was in the room. Then, every time they looked at the Special Ed. poster they'd be looking at somebody's nosepicking, and they might not even see it, but it would be there. I'd know. It would serve them right.

Serve who right?

He couldn't think of the answer.

Then he looked at the other wall, with the Going Up party pictures on it. If you walked right over to it and looked close, you'd see Shana and Nick with their mouths open wide, laughing, with the balloon above both their heads, but you wouldn't know Shana was holding his hand, because they were behind two other kids kneeling on the grass. It looked as if their arms were just hanging down at their sides.

Then there was the bendy blondish hair on his desk, and nobody knew about that. Except if you could count Dianne. He didn't know if you could count her.

Maybe God was laughing at him all this time. For trying to count Dianne in thinking.

There was nobody you could ask. Not in the world, even.

What if you asked Dianne who was the president right now and she didn't know? That wouldn't be her fault, she was dead. She couldn't know about the president, she couldn't even know about the things last year. Dianne wouldn't even know about getting her period or anything.

And another thing: if you brought Dianne in here right now and asked her, Where is your little brother? she wouldn't even know. Nick was a little kid then.

Dianne didn't even know what he looked like.

A horrible feeling began in his stomach. All those things I've been trying to ask Dianne—she doesn't even know who's asking. He wanted to say HELP in the loudest voice he had, but he was in school, and it was time to go to Tuesday science. Good: he could work on amphibians there.

Mr. Wakamatsu in Tuesday science got a kick out of Nick remembering "batrachian" for amphibians without tails. Only two other kids in the class knew it without asking, Mr. Wakamatsu said. Nick was the only Room 19 one in Tuesday science, and he had no problem there except reading and spelling the words, and Mr. Wakamatsu said that wasn't the most important thing, anyway. Nick was a fair speller for Room 19 but a rotten speller for everyplace else.

"Nick, I've got a great one for you today," Mr. Wakamatsu said when Nick walked into the lab. "Wait till you see this baby. It's the Midwife Toad." He held out a big book, open. She had little bubbles all over her back. "Guess what that stuff on his back is." The teacher was really excited.

"Eggs. And it's her back, not his. Does she do that till they hatch?" You could tell they were eggs, in their soft jelly sacs.

"You're partly right. But this is the male. I'm not kidding. The female attaches the eggs to his hind legs, and he takes care of them, he carries them around till hatching time. Isn't that a nice arrangement?"

"Boy, it sure is. Are you sure that's the male?"

"I'm sure. Look in the slide catalog and you'll find more of them. They live in France, Portugal, and places—not around here." He wrote the name of the toad on a piece of paper so Nick could look it up.

Nick memorized some things about the Midwife Toad: two to three inches long, gray or brown back, red or green spots, the male hides in a hole while the eggs mature, and he only comes out at night, to eat and get the eggs wet.

Then he started on the Pig Frog, which has maybe the best tympanum of any frog, it's big, with a partly whitish ring around it. The whole Pig Frog is a beautiful color, lime green. They named it Pig Frog because it sounds like a pig. People can eat the legs and it croaks all year long, usually floating. The tadpoles get to be five inches long and it takes them two whole years to transform. Nick looked at three Pig Frog slides. It has a huge sacral hump, and it's even pretty, too, the hump, because it's the same lime green color as the rest of it. The Pig Frog lives in the southern United States, and it sometimes grows to almost seven inches. Nick knew all that, but he always liked to go back to that frog, one of the prettiest of all the frogs, with that sad, ugly name.

"Nick, here's another critter for you, it's right here in Oregon—in fact, it's only in Oregon and Washington, only in the Columbia Gorge. Isn't it pretty?" Mr. Wakamatsu was talking to him, and Nick looked up from the Pig Frog slide.

"Here, look. And by the way, when are you gonna get tired of the Pig Frog?"

"I don't know, I like it. I'd like to see one real."

The teacher had a book open to a salamander with an orange back stripe and a nice black line down the center. "This one they don't even know very much about yet. They don't know exactly how it breeds or anything. It's the Larch Mountain, and you could probably see it if you went there—"

"Yeah, if I went there and stayed quiet for about a year."

"Your record is perfect, Nick. All year, you've never made one bad joke. This guy runs about three or four inches—and they don't even know for absolute sure about that. It lives among the Douglas fir on Larch Mountain, they think it likes the lava soil. It's the only Woodland with red on its belly and the underside of its feet and tail—they think. Wouldn't it be fun to find one?"

"Sure. Wait—how many costal grooves does it have?"

"Nick, do you know you're the only person in the class who always asks that? Let's count." They counted, and allowed for some hidden by the legs in the photograph. About fifteen.

Sort of average for a salamander. But Nick agreed it was kind of exciting that Oregon had its own sal, the Larch Mountain. Maybe it just evolved in Oregon all by itself, millions of years ago. It had to, it had to come out of the water, of course it wasn't a salamander yet, it was still a sort of fish, with gills. Think of learning to breathe on land. It took so many generations, you couldn't even imagine.

Imagine God planning all that evolution. Imagine thinking it all up.

Nick was putting in his memory: Larch Mountain Sal, breeding not known for sure, up to four inches, orange stripe with black center line, fifteen costal grooves, and his mind switched. He was going to the prom. He had a date. Her name was Shana, she'd wear a lavender dress with flowers on the material. He grinned at the Larch Mountain Sal.

The lavender dress would be so pretty. Shana used to wear old jeans and sweatshirts to school some of the time in Room 19, but already she had two new sweaters, a medium blue one and a pink one. And she wasn't even hanging around with Jill and Becky very much anymore, he thought. Maybe he was wrong. But it seemed as if just Jill and Becky had lunch together now.

Midwife Toad, Pig Frog, Larch Mountain Salamander. Next week he'd eat lunch with Shana, like a second date.

Dianne would go steady with the football captain now, or somebody like that. She'd go on dates to movies and everything, with some big guy driving a car.

He sat in the lab looking at salamanders and thinking about how Special Ed. made a difference with cars. You had to memorize the whole driving book, but you couldn't do that if you couldn't read it. They had the driving book on tape, and Mr. Norton worked on it with him, but only on Wednesday, and it was hard to remember from one Wednesday to the next one. Mr. Norton laughed when the kids called the license bureau The Old Sock It To 'Em Bureau. He said, "Think of the people who just came from Cambodia—imagine them trying to get drivers' licenses; the whole thing is almost impossible. You're not weird, the license bureau is weird. Wait till you have to read the income tax form—*I* can't even read it."

But the football players and those guys had drivers' licenses.

He looked at the Santa Cruz Salamander and suddenly thought of Mrs. Rosenbaum. In sixth grade, or maybe it was fifth, Mrs. Rosenbaum said something like "Everybody's different. Somebody's different in China and somebody's different because they have diabetes and insulin. Somebody's different with a pacemaker in their heart, somebody can't see colors except gray. Do you know Beethoven couldn't do math?"

Nobody in the class knew what Mrs. Rosenbaum was talking about.

"Beethoven, he's dead now, he made symphonies, he was the greatest composer in the world, he couldn't do math, he wasn't even a good dancer. Everybody's different. You're just different in reading. And things like that."

Mrs. Rosenbaum giggled, as if everything she said was true except little parts of it. She wore a frilly blouse, and she patted the frilly part when she giggled. She giggled when she said "and things like that."

Maybe Mrs. Rosenbaum was seventh grade. Maybe that

wasn't even exactly what she said. But she was trying to explain Special Ed.

Nick was sixteen and he could drive a car to the prom, they had two cars, except he was Special Ed. and he didn't know how to drive. His dad gave him two lessons once, he could back out of the garage, but that wasn't real driving.

The bell rang.

Along with the car problem was the problem of parents. You could say a lot of things about parents, in fact you could write a book about parents if you were a book writer. Nick had fairly good parents, but they were still a problem. Sometimes he could look at them and feel sorry for them, and sometimes he looked at them and wondered how they could be so ridiculous.

Like the telephone call. On the night of day four until day zero. First Nick's mother had a conversation with Shana's mother, then his father had a conversation with Shana's father, then they all talked together on four phones in two houses, it was a long phone call. You couldn't even believe the things they figured out to talk about. But finally they decided that his parents would take him to the hotel where the prom was, and Shana's parents would take her there. Then Nick's dad would pick them both up and take them to the marina for the boat ride. Then after the boat ride, Shana's father would bring them home. His parents didn't even know Shana's parents at all, but they talked a long time. It made Nick feel funny, like people looking into your room and deciding things about the way you had your room arranged.

At the last of the phone call, his father stayed quiet, not talking for a long time, and then he said, "Yes, yes it is. Very."

Then there was another silence. Then he said, "Yes it is. Yes it is. Very."

His father talked that way sometimes. Isn't that a good report card? Yes, yes it is. Very. Isn't that typical of the government? Yes, yes it is. Very. It meant he was thinking and he didn't want you to know very much of his thinking.

Then, after everybody hung up, his dad walked straight over to Nick, who was going through the dining room on his way to take Patsy outside for a walk, and he put his whole arm around Nick, and he said, "Go for it, son."

Nick said okay. He had no idea what his father meant by it. It was like saying okay to a thunderstorm, or to buying a new pair of shoes. You just said it, you didn't know what was up.

His mind was on practicing dancing. As he dropped six socks and his math book and two shirts on the floor in front of the mirror for his seventeenth lesson, he said, Okay, Dianne, you're laughing, probably.

Dianne, I wish we could go on a double date. You might wear a blue dress, you'd be tall, you'd have your big, thick red braids down the back of the blue dress, your football guy would hold your hand, we'd laugh after dark together, and if he made fun of Special Ed. you'd knock him in the teeth. Dianne, you're a great sister.

The song ended. Nick was dancing with a pillow.

3

On the day of the prom, day zero, Nick had a long list of things to do. No worry about the tuxedo rental, they delivered. They knew his size, they knew the color of shirt, blue, they knew his legs, they knew how tall he was, five feet and eleven inches, they knew everything they needed.

He had to practice dancing some more, and he had to make sure the boat ride tickets were together with the prom tickets in his pocket. He had to have a haircut, his mother said she never went to a prom with a boy who didn't have a haircut. Mothers were old, but this was probably right. (Probably, again.)

He had to walk Patsy, twice, he had to wash both his mom's and his dad's cars, even though he wouldn't be driving to the prom. He had to go on his bike to the florist for the wrist corsage of pink rosebuds and then take it on his bike to Shana's house. She'd be surprised. Of course she expected a corsage, but maybe she didn't expect a wrist corsage, and maybe she didn't expect pink rosebuds.

He had to work with the braces on his teeth, he had to make sure there was nothing caught in them. He had to take a shower. And he had to shave, probably twice. They never warned you about how hard it was to shave, they never told you you might have to do it twice.

The day was long and hot, nice May weather. When he wasn't busy with the haircut or with the other things, he worked with the amphibian chart, memorizing more names and characteristics: the Northern Dusky Sal, and the Mountain Dusky with all its different kinds, all with different patterns of orange.

Just after one o'clock, he set out on his bike for the florist. One of the things he didn't know was: Do you call the florist first, to make sure the flowers are ready? He didn't know, so he got on his bike and went there.

Boy, he could almost pass the driving test right now. Backing the car out of the garage and putting it back in the garage, those things were easy compared to moving a ten-speed in and out of traffic. And little kids are always wanting to cross the street before their parents are ready to, when you ride a bike in traffic you always see these grown-up arms slamming out in the middle of the air, trying to keep the little kids from dashing into the side of some car. Little kids are really dangerous.

He wheeled his bike right into the shop with him, and a lady with tall silver hair behind the counter looked at him as if he was a big dog that was going to knock over the buckets of flowers.

She doesn't know I work in the greenhouse, he thought. Nick smiled in his head and walked his bike straight to the counter, and he asked her for the wrist corsage of pink rose-buds with just the little bit of baby's breath, and he told the lady his name.

She sent a boy to find the corsage while she frowned at Nick's bike. His bike was perfectly centered between rows of buckets and plant stands, and he was holding it steady.

The boy brought the corsage: You could tell they'd been picked just right, picked when they should be. The buds were tight and healthy, with the leaves not looking old or tired. Portland, Oregon, City of Roses.

"This for your girlfriend?" The lady's eyes opened wide, either excited or pretending to be excited.

I don't know, I don't know, I don't know. I don't think she's my girlfriend, but I don't know. You don't have any right to ask me. I don't know. He didn't say anything.

"Big dance tonight?" the lady asked.

"Yes," Nick said. He pulled out the money from his pocket and handed it to her.

"I bet she's pretty," the lady said, and took his money. While she made the change, she kept talking. "Is she gonna wear a pink dress? I bet she'll be gorgeous."

"No. Lavender." That was one question he could answer. It would be a lavender dress, with flowers on the material. "She made it herself, with her mother, on the sewing machine." Nick couldn't explain it, but he felt proud of Shana sewing her own dress. Anybody could go and buy a dress, if they had the money or if they could work at a job to earn the money, but Shana sewed hers. That must be really hard to do.

The lady's hair was piled high on her head, it looked as

if it might fall if she got too excited. She counted out the change and put it in Nick's hand. "She made her own dress—my, my, she must be very creative. Goodness sakes."

Creative. Maybe so. Nick didn't know.

"I don't know," he said.

The lady looked at him in a way that made him feel he'd made a wrong answer. Then she said, "Well, you have a good time now, at the dance. I bet she'll just love the flowers."

He couldn't help smiling at her, even though she had that look on her face for a little while. "Yeah. I bet she will."

He put the corsage, in its box, in the left wire basket on the back of his bike and wheeled the bike backward out of the shop, very carefully. The lady watched him all the way out of the shop. When he got to the doorway, and got the door open and the bike out, he turned around and waved to the lady. He couldn't have explained why, he just decided to wave to her. She waved back, almost looking surprised. And the way she waved was funny: It was the way you wave at a little kid, moving your fingers up and down together, instead of sideways. It was the kind of wave you wanted to say bye-bye with, the way first graders say bye-bye in that little bony voice.

He couldn't think about it now, he had to work the bike onto the street and get to Shana's house before the flowers got too warm; they had to go in the refrigerator right away.

Shana lived about twenty blocks from his house in an old house her parents were fixing up. Nick checked his watch when he had to stop at the first red light, and he checked it again when he made the right turn onto Shana's street, and it was sixteen minutes and fourteen seconds. Not bad.

He recognized the house from the time Jason Bartholomew's mother had driven everybody home from a track meet one day. It had ladders and paint cans all around it, and sawhorses and old boards and new ones, and it smelled like people working with paint. Nick left his bike in the driveway, took the corsage box out of the back basket, and walked to what he thought was the front door. It turned out to be the back door. He knocked.

The lady who came to the door must be Shana's mother. She looked at him as if he was a stranger, not very friendly. "Yes?" she said.

She had on jeans with light blue and orange and white paint spots all over them, and a floppy orange T-shirt with a ragged bottom. She was in bare feet.

Nick held up the box with the corsage in it. "This is for Shana." He knew he should say something else. He couldn't remember what it was.

The lady tilted her head way back and looked at the ceiling and then brought her head back down fast. "You must be Nicholas! Why, Nicholas, how sweet of you to drop by!" She reached her hand out, he was supposed to shake her hand and say, How do you do, and he was holding the box, and he put the box in her hand instead, and she took it and laughed, "Oh, how wonderful, I bet I know what's in here! I'm Mrs. Kerby, how do you do, Nicholas? Would you like to come in? We're just in the middle of— please come in, Shana's not home, we're a mess around here, how nice to meet you, Nicholas!"

Nick remembered a word from school, they had to learn the word so they'd be patient with some kids in sixth grade: hyperactive. Those were the kids who couldn't sit still or keep still, and the teacher made you learn about it so you could stand being in the same room with them.

Shana's mother might be one of the hyperactives, some people never get completely over it, it's in their chemicals, and you're just patient with them, that's all.

"Come in, Nicholas, we're working on the kitchen, see, we took out this wall, and we moved it back to there, and we took out that wall—well, you can't really see that—and, oh—this is Ms. Sugarman, and this is Mr. Marcher, they're just taking a few pictures of the kitchen. Ms. Sugarman, Mr. Marcher, this is Nicholas, Shana's friend from school, Nicholas rode here on his bike, didn't you, Nicholas? Mr. Marcher and Ms. Sugarman are just taking some pictures for a magazine, let's—"

Nick didn't want to interrupt, you shouldn't interrupt the hyperactives because they had to keep going, but he had to. She was pointing all over the place, and the corsage box was going up and down in her hand, waving, and you could tell the rosebuds were bumping into the sides of the box, and Piglet and Pooh and Eeyore's birthday presents came into his mind again.

"Mrs. Kerby, the corsage has to go in the refrigerator, so the—"

"Of course! We'll put it in the refrigerator, isn't this a dandy?"

Nick looked. The refrigerator door was transparent. Through it, you could see carrots, lettuce, melons, and casseroles and milk and butter and eggs, and at the top you could see the ice cubes, falling into a container. He'd never seen anything like it in his life. A refrigerator door you could see through. It was amazing.

Mrs. Kerby opened the transparent door and put the corsage box on the third shelf, next to a bunch of fresh celery. "We'll keep it right here till Shana comes home, now would you like to see the rest?"

He had to go home and take a shower and shave and practice dancing, but you couldn't say no to one of the hyperactives very well, so he said yes.

"This wall used to be—well, it used to be a wall, and we pushed it back twelve feet, and here's the cooking island"— it was blue tile, it seemed to go on for miles—"and here's the range"—it was a stove with no burners, but some pink marks in circles showed where you might cook—"and you should've seen what we had to do here, we—well, this is what we came up with—" Mrs. Kerby stopped. You could walk around in that kitchen without ever bumping into the potted trees or the paintings with orange frames, if you wanted to. You could maybe even roller-skate all around it. One painting was of red tulips about three feet tall.

"Boy, those tulips are tall," Nick said, pointing.

"Oh, yes, aren't they marvelous? That's a print from our friend, she's shown in three galleries, these are her tulips, aren't they wonderful, the—they go with the wallpaper wonderfully, don't they? You should've seen the—well, it was, oh, it was just such a job, and the—excuse me, excuse me, Nicholas, Ms. Sugarman wants an angle here—"

She shoved him out of the way, not hard, and Ms. Sugarman moved in with her camera, and behind Ms. Sugarman a man walked in from somewhere and said,

"Socks. Where're my socks? Anybody do laundry around here?"

Mrs. Kerby laughed and said, "Yesssss. Somebody does. On top of the dryer. Larry darling, this is Nicholas, Shana's friend from school, he rode here on his bike."

This is Mr. Kerby, Nick decided. He was a little bit fat, not very fat, and he had a sort of bald head, and he was in shorts and bare feet, they must not like shoes around this house, but he wanted socks.

"Larry darling, say hello to Nicho—"

But the man was gone, through a doorway, after nodding his head at Nick. Through the doorway, Nick could see another room that looked as if nobody had lived there for years. Boxes were piled high, and ladders and paint cans were all over the floor.

The room he was looking into was gloomy, dark. A sewing machine was near a window, that was why Nick could see it, and it had a tall lamp beside it, standing on the floor.

"Excuse us, Nicholas, Ms. Sugarman wants to move here, I'm sorry to inconvenience—"

"I gotta go home," Nick heard himself saying.

"Oh, of course, you've got a big night ahead, it was so nice of—"

"The flowers, they're for Shana," he reminded her.

"Oh, yes, they're wonderful, they're in the refrigerator. . . ."

"Next to the celery," Nick said.

"Right! You're wonderful! Oops, excuse me, Mr. Marcher, there we are—oh, this corner didn't used to be here . . . now, there we are, can you find your way out, Nicholas . . . oh, there's a—all right, that's fine—there was a—but you got right over it, isn't the blue wonderful with the orange and the—oops, watch—the counter, thanks for coming by, Nicholas. . . ."

Nick found his way among sawhorses and ladders to the driveway and got on his bike, turned it around in the driveway, and started for home.

So that was the room where Shana made the lavender dress. And that kitchen she had her breakfast in. Very strange family. He pedaled home.

When he got home, his mother was sitting at the kitchen table, reading a magazine, and a record was playing. She was drinking tea from a mug that said Free Lunch. She was in charge of getting food from restaurants and stores for the poor people, that must be why she could have a mug to take home. She looked up. "Home again, sweetheart? How was traffic?"

Traffic was fine. But you should see Shana's mother. "Okay," he said. He started to go upstairs to his room.

Her music was loud, and he had to practice dancing. "Hey, Mom, could you turn that music down? It's loud," he said.

"Nick, do you know what that music is? It's Beethoven. It's the song about joy, the last part of the Ninth Symphony. I don't know, I guess it's almost against some kind of rule to play it soft. . . ." But she turned it down.

"Thanks," he said.

He went to his room and turned on the radio to find dance music. He'd just found a station with the right kind when his mother interrupted him, knocking on his door.

"Nick, Beethoven was completely deaf when he wrote that symphony. Did I ever tell you that?"

"I don't know."

"Well, he was. He couldn't hear, he never even heard that symphony in his life. And he still wrote it with the chorus of joy at the end. Isn't that amazing?"

"Yeah." You had to say that to make your mother happy, but it really was amazing if you thought about it.

"He just heard the music in his brain, inside. No ear hearing. I think it's one of the most amazing things in the world." She started to close his door.

"Yeah, Mom, it really is." You had to keep making your mother happy. He turned up the volume of the radio.

Nick studied amphibians and practiced dancing for the rest of the afternoon. The Large-blotched Salamander looks as if somebody sewed it crooked up the back, its markings don't exactly meet, it lives at Mt. Palomar and other places in California.

What if there's a song so fast you can't dance to it, what do you do then? If she wants to hold your hand, how long do you hold it, her hand? The Sierra Nevada Sal, twelve or thirteen costal grooves, has a stiff-legged defense posture and orange blotches. In slow dancing, where do you put your head, is it okay for it to go at the place where her ear is, one of her ears, let's see: her right one? The Sierra Nevada is one kind of Ensatina. There are about six other kinds.

No wonder his parents stayed on the phone with Shana's parents so long. Her mother, anyway. And his.

If you knew about Down's syndrome you wouldn't get mad at the Down's kids in Room 19, if you knew about hyperactive you wouldn't get mad at Shana's mother. The Leopard Frog lives in more different places in North America than any other amphibian. It has night eyeshine.

The rented tuxedo arrived. It had so many parts. That was another thing you couldn't ask anybody: How do you do a tuxedo?

All your life, people told you not to be scared. They acted as if fear was something you shouldn't get, like dirty or drunk. Don't get dirty, don't get drunk, don't get hurt, don't get scared.

Girls could get scared a little bit, and boys not at all. Even girls weren't supposed to. Look at Dianne, she wasn't scared.

But at the last. How she must have got scared. Don't think about it.

Now, you had to learn how to use a tuxedo, and you couldn't say you were scared, or you'd get the same old thing again: Don't get scared. Or like Mr. Norton: "Nothing to it. Trust me."

Things could go wrong. You could fasten something wrong, and people could look at you and laugh. He stood in his room and looked at the tuxedo hanging in the plastic bag, with the hanger hooked over the top of his closet door. He looked at Patsy and told her he was scared. She hung her tongue out and smiled.

He didn't say anything about it during dinner. His dad wanted to tell him at dinner that the prom was a right of passage. He said it was spelled r-i-t-e, and it was like the way some tribes send guys out all alone into the jungle or the forest and they have to do certain things, like kill an animal or have a dream or vision or something, and when they come back they're not boys anymore, they're men, it's like a ceremony.

"Did they do that to you?" Nick asked his dad.

His dad laughed. "Sure, son, lots of times." His father stayed quiet for a little while, eating chicken.

His mother smiled. "I know one time . . ." she sang, kind of in a little tune.

"Which one?" his dad asked.

"No fair. I'll tell after you tell," she said.

"Okay, let's see. One was not making the football team. One was falling down ice-skating on my very first date. One was dropping the collection plate in church. One was—this is the worst one—telling your grandpa I wanted to be a dentist, not a lawyer. Grandpa was fierce that time—remember, Marsh?"

She laughed. "He just stood in the middle of the room and said, 'Dentist—dentist—*den*tist. . . .' He just kept saying it, over and over again. Poor man."

Nick couldn't see what was wrong with being a dentist, and his parents agreed. There was nothing wrong with being a dentist at all, Grandpa was the one wrong.

"Which one were you thinking of?" his dad said to his mother.

She was still laughing. "Meeting my parents."

"Right! Good afternoon, Mr. and Mrs. Lawrence. My name is Ralph Swansen and my father's cut me out of his will for not going to law school, and your daughter gets better grades in history than I do—and I didn't make the football team, and I dropped the collection plate once, and I can't stay on my feet in ice skates and I want to marry your daughter. . . ."

Nick's mother leaned forward. "Dad didn't really say all that, dear. But it was pretty funny. Your grandparents mostly just sat and stared at him."

"Just sat. And stared. That was one big rite of passage," his dad said. His mother and dad laughed, it must be one big joke for old people.

Nick wanted to ask. About the tuxedo. About what part of it you put on first. And if you could dance in it—well, of course you could, or they wouldn't make tuxedos. And could you take off the jacket if it got hot at the dance? And that belt thing, the light blue, shiny thing that almost matched the shirt.

Were you just supposed to know those things? He excused himself from the table to take a shower. He shaved twice, without cutting his face at all. Maybe that was good luck. And maybe it wasn't.

His dad walked into his room just exactly at the time he was sitting on his bed staring at the rented tuxedo. "I ever tell you about the first time I wore a tux?" His dad was laughing. "I had no idea what went where, and my brother showed me. I don't think I'd ever have figured it out by myself. Mind if I help?"

"No," Nick said.

His dad went to the closet door and started taking the whole complicated thing out of the plastic bag. "I bet it's like girls figuring out garter belts and stuff like that," he laughed. Nick knew garter belts from the book Bruce brought to school, a catalog of lace underwear and other things, with ladies standing by curtains or sitting on beds.

It was probably true, girls probably did have to figure them out the first time. But, with probably things, you didn't really know.

His dad got him into it, the tuxedo. Straps, and stripes, one down the side of each leg, and buttons, and the wide belt was called a cummerbund and it came from the Hindus that wore them first, and the bow tie was no problem when his dad attached it.

Then his dad made him march down the stairs, wearing the whole thing, and he made his mother come into the living room with her eyes closed, to surprise her. It was a kids' game, but his dad was getting a kick out of it, so Nick went along with it.

When his mother opened her eyes, she got tears in them right away. "Oh, Nick, you look great," she said. Mothers were ridiculous, but they couldn't help it. "Shouldn't we take pictures?" Absolutely ridiculous.

"I thought I'd take the camera when I go to pick them up and take them to the marina, that way I can get Shana in the picture," his dad said.

The parents were being the kids, Nick thought, but he said okay. He and Shana already had pictures together one time, this would make two. He stopped thinking about it so he wouldn't get nervous. Maybe the nervousness was because of his braces. He went to the downstairs bathroom to brush his teeth again. Was this four times? He laughed: Brushing your teeth four times—that was something you'd never tell anybody.

"Well, who's gonna drive this trip?" his dad asked in the living room after the fourth toothbrushing. "Shall we flip a coin?" Nick looked at himself in the living room window, really six small windows making up a big one. He was divided in parts, somebody in a tuxedo with lines going through him to make him into parts.

His mother wanted to drive him to the prom, she wasn't just pretending, you could tell. "I really want to, okay, dear? I don't know, I just want to be there. I haven't been to a prom in—I don't know, more than twenty years." She had her purse and keys ready.

"And for that prom, your date had been cut out of his father's will because of dental school, and he was rather a handsome specimen, too, right?" Nick's father was really being childish.

"Right, my dear. And you still are." His mother had her keys in her hand, kind of hanging in the air, and she stopped, her arm dangling the keys. They clinked. "You still are," she said, and got little tears in her eyes again. This was really immature.

Nick knew exactly where the prom tickets were, and the tickets for the boat ride, he'd paid his I.O.U. with greenhouse money. He and his mother got into the car.

She wanted to talk about proms during the drive to the hotel, about the yellow dress she wore that time, and Nick partly listened, his mind was on his own questions, they were questions you couldn't ask your mother.

"Wouldn't you? Hey, Nick, wake up. Wouldn't you?" She was nudging him.

He hadn't heard. "What?" he asked. You had to be polite.

"I said, Daddy couldn't afford a corsage, he knew I'd be wearing a yellow dress, and he went all over the hills picking just yellow and blue and purple wildflowers—it was really hard to find them in May and he found them, he gave me this bouquet, you couldn't wear it on a dress—but it was this bouquet, it had violets in it, and yellow, I think they were buttercups. It was this beautiful bouquet from the hills, all wildflowers. And I said it was lovely, because it *was* lovely. Wouldn't you?"

"Sure."

"So. The next morning, he called me and asked me if I'd let him take me to breakfast, and I said yes, and we had waffles at this funny little restaurant. And I took along the bouquet and I stuck it in a water glass on the table."

"That's nice, Mom." He looked at her. She was driving with a really happy look on her face.

"I pressed two of the flowers in a book. I still have them," she said.

They got to the hotel where the prom was. "Listen, Nick, you have a good time. Don't worry about anything— anything, okay? Just have a great, great time. You've earned a good time," she said.

"In the greenhouse," Nick said. He got out of the car.

"Right dear. And other places. I won't see you till tomorrow. Good night, sweetheart."

"Yeah. Good night. Thanks." He closed the car door.

She drove away, Nick watched the people arriving for the prom and looked for Shana. She wasn't there yet. It was okay, he'd wait.

They could make fun of you for being Special Ed. and letting your mother bring you to the prom, but there were lots of Special Ed. kids who never went to a prom in their whole lives.

Nick waited and watched girls in long dresses and guys in rented tuxedos go in the big doors.

He waited. Shana would get there soon, she'd wear the pink wrist corsage, she'd wear a lavender dress. It was getting cold. She should be here any minute.

4

When his watch said 10:03 P.M., Nick knew he was cold. Oregon weather: hot days, cold nights. You could tell the wind was coming up off the Columbia River and moving around the corners of the hotel. Probably Shana's parents were changing a flat tire right now, and it wouldn't be fair to go inside the hotel just to get a cup of hot chocolate when Shana was sitting in her prom dress and wrist corsage in a car beside the road with the flashers on.

His mother said that when your feet are cold the rest of you is cold, and when your feet are warm the rest of you is warm. Then it was his feet, of course. You could dance, and warm your feet that way.

You had to have music. If he moved out of the window light, nobody would see him dancing, but there wouldn't be any music. He had to make a decision because he was cold. Could he make up music? If you could do that, you might as well be Beethoven.

Wait a minute. He knew a song, where your right foot

jumps and your left foot slides, up against the "–bee" in "You're all I got to love baybee tonight." And he knew you could turn it around, you could jump with your left foot and slide with the right one, and it wouldn't make any difference if nobody was watching. It was hard to start the song, though. But he was cold, and he decided to try to dance in the shadows over there where the cars were parked. He could keep watching for when Shana and her parents would come into the driveway of the hotel.

So he moved into the shadows. It felt even colder there, but he knew it was just his imagination. He tried to hear the song in his head. It was something about "I like your hair the way it grows down to there," and there was some more about lonely and only. You dug your hips in where the words went "Stay with me I want you to play with me baby tonight." He'd start there.

It was weird to be moving his legs without a mirror, he couldn't tell if he was really dancing or just moving. But it would warm up his ears if he kept doing it, so he did. Shana would be here soon, and it would be terrible if he had cold hands for when he wanted to put them on her shoulders and tell her how her dress was so pretty.

His feet moved pretty well for a parking lot: "You've got such pretty lips I like the way you move your hips stay with me baybee tonight." He decided he was actually dancing, and now he wasn't so cold.

He could just about remember the song "Something about your waist something about your taste stay with me baby tonight," and his feet went between two cars. He couldn't see them reflected in the hubcaps, but he knew they were doing fine.

He was warmed up, and he decided to sit on the hotel's front steps and wait for Shana. Boy, she was late. In her pretty dress, she must be really ready to dance.

Her parents would say how long it took to change the flat tire, and Shana would—oh, boy—he hadn't planned how he would take her arm when she was getting out of the car, probably the backseat. He'd just reach out his arm—wait a minute—which one, left or right? He was glad he had time to figure it out now; he imagined himself against the car, and decided it was the left arm he should put there. Boy, it was good they were late; he might not have figured it out if they'd gotten there on time.

Nick went over the things they'd talk about while they danced. School, and next year, and their summer jobs. He'd be working at the nursery for the summer, watering plants and taking care of them, transplanting and weeding and the rest of the stuff. Shana was going to work at the day camp, she'd look so pretty helping the little kids and making them laugh.

Now he was bored again. When you're bored, invent a math problem and work it out, Mr. Norton said. He always said, Don't make it an impossible one. Nick decided to invent how far the hose would reach in the nursery to water all the plants without having to be hooked up more than two different places. He remembered the faucets and he figured it out, the eight rows of plants, fast.

Boy, my butt's cold, he thought. My butt's cold, my butt's cold, the Room 19 kids would make a song out of that. Boy, I hope I get to go Up out of Room 19 someday.

He looked inside through the tall windows. Couples were standing at the sides of the ballroom. They must be getting ready to crown the queen. I'll be able to tell Shana how they stood at the sides, she'll want to know. He kept looking and looking, and the parade started, with the prom princesses and their escorts walking in a line. One of the princesses would be queen and get her picture in the year-book.

He watched the crown get put on the queen's head, it was made of shiny stones with some flowers on it, and the girls kissed, the queen and some other girl. It was all pink with lights and then the band started playing again and nobody danced but the queen and her date. He was a quarterback. The quarterback looked kind of silly, kind of like somebody in a wrong place, all wound up in a purple cummerbund inside the tuxedo jacket. The different kinds of shoes people could wear was kind of an interesting thing, too: spikes for football and very fancy tuxedo shoes for dancing.

Then everybody else started dancing. It was really crowded now, and the slow dancing had guys' hands on girls' hips, just the way he'd practiced with a pillow in the mirror, remembering not to push too hard because of the dress Shana made on the sewing machine. You wouldn't want to crush it.

He wondered if the flowers on Shana's dress looked like growing ones, or like ones just laid on the dress. She said it had flowers on it.

Now, suddenly, Nick knew he was angry. He couldn't figure out what he was angry at, though. You couldn't be angry at somebody's car for having a flat tire or maybe having some other kind of problem, spark plugs or something. If Shana was sitting in the car by the side of the road and wanting the car not to have problems, you couldn't be angry at her.

Maybe he was angry at Jason Bartholomew about the amphibians, Jason said they didn't evolve and God made them just the way they are now, even though the Smithonian man on TV said they evolved and Mr. Wakamatsu in Tuesday science had charts and lessons about evolving. Jason said Nick was crazy, Jason said too that it wasn't Smithonian, it was Smithsonian, with another "s" in it. Jason bunched up his fist and said he was right, Smithonian man or no Smithonian man.

Nick kept trying to ask Mr. Wakamatsu about the other "s," but when he was talking to Mr. Wakamatsu he forgot, and when he remembered, Mr. Wakamatsu was leaning over somebody else's microscope or something. Nick was just a guest in Tuesday science anyway. Jason didn't get to go to Tuesday science, and he said he didn't even want to, Mr. Wakamatsu was the heathen. That's what Jason Bartholomew said.

Nick promised himself to make a mind note to ask about Smithonian or Smithsonian. Mr. Norton was big on mind notes, but they didn't always work. "Make mind notes to yourself. Test yourself after twenty-four hours, try to remember what the note was yesterday at that time. If you make a mind note on Tuesday at three o'clock, ask yourself on Wednesday at three o'clock to say the mind note out loud. That's one kind of smartness. Everybody in Room 19 can be smart, it's just a matter of figuring out the right questions to ask. Everybody has to do it. Make a mind note of that. I'll ask you in twenty-four hours what I said."

Everybody laughed. The next day, sure enough, Mr. Norton said, "What did I say twenty-four hours ago?"

Nick didn't know, but Jill and Shana did. Shana even knew it by memory, every single word. "Everybody in Room 19 can be smart, it's just a matter of figuring out the right questions to ask. Everybody has to do it. Make a mind note of that. I'll ask you in twenty-four hours what I said."

She looked like a show-off, sitting in her chair with her legs crossed, swinging one foot up and down. The kids were right about that. Bruce and Alex especially made fun of her for looking like a show-off. But they didn't say "stupid show-off." You couldn't say words like "stupid" or "dumb" or "moron" in Room 19. Mr. Norton's rule.

That was one of the reasons Shana got to go Up mainstreamed, then: She could remember almost everything they were learning in Room 19. She also did a lot of homework, and she thought paper airplanes were childish.

Nick's watch said 11:18, and he was cold again. Poor Shana wasn't going to get very much dancing done tonight. Their car must have terrible trouble.

Now the band was playing a fast dance. Nick decided he should maybe go to the parking lot again, to dance and warm up. He started to take his nearly shivering self off the steps. Just in time.

The doors opened and two men in tuxedos came out, one lighting a cigarette. Nick hid behind a column; he'd feel weird walking toward the parking lot, and they might ask him what he was doing.

"Those dummies don't know when to stop," one of the men said. "If I danced all night like that, I'd have a coronary. Good thing chaperons don't have to do anything, just be there."

"Right. Nice dance, though. Lindy looks wonderful in her crown. How do you like having a prom queen in the family?" the other man said.

"This makes two. Her sister was, three years ago. Takes some getting over, but it's not fatal. She'll be hard to live with for about a week, that's all. Minute school's out, she's a working gal. I got her a computer job down at the place; she's dynamite at computers. Smart gal, we're proud of her."

"Yep, you can be proud of her, all right. Dynamite dancer, too. One round with me, she was ready to go again—and I needed something stronger than that punch they've got in there."

Both men laughed.

The prom queen's father said, "Your boys are gonna graduate too, right? What're their plans? Going to college? Oh—stupid of me. One of the boys has a sort of—sorry I asked. Well, big strong—"

"No, it's okay. Ron, he's going to UCLA, and Jon, he's gonna take some time figuring out what he wants to do. Oh, smart as a whip, but—well, just sort of a problem in math and like that. He's a good kid, good as they come."

The taller one, the prom queen's father, took a puff of the cigarette. It lit his face and showed him frowning. "Oh, sure, they're both great kids." He blew smoke into the air, aiming upward. "Tell me, Howie, isn't it true that with identical twins—"

"Yeah, that's it. Sometimes, not always. We got it, other families didn't. Oh, he's not that bad—"

"No, sure, not that bad at all. Taken all regular classes, hasn't he? No Special Ed. or anything like that?"

"Right. Kept him in regular classes, kept him on his toes. Not a big problem. After they tried tutoring, they wanted to put him in Special Ed., you know, just for a kind of catch-up. But I said no. No son of mine's gonna sit with the droolers. They finally saw it my way. It'd be a handicap. You put a kid with the droolers, he'll end up a drooler."

"Exactly. It's their self-concept of themselves. That's the most important thing. You think Jon can work in at one of the stores, then?"

"Sure. With three of them, we can find him something. Probably at the west side branch. He's got great potential, just hasn't worked up to it yet. Kids have to learn to concentrate. Schools today don't teach 'em to concentrate, that's the problem."

The men nodded at each other, and the prom queen's father dropped his cigarette and stepped on it. "Well, looks like they're winding down in there," he said. "You and Joan want to come over for a drink?"

"Great idea. These kids are gonna go their own sweet way, anyway."

The door opened, the men laughed and put their hands on each other's shoulders and went back into the ballroom. As they walked inside, the music and warm air waved out smoothly, reaching Nick where he stood behind the column. He felt very, very cold now.

He couldn't imagine ever learning to talk the way the two chaperons talked. They knew so much, they didn't stop between words and look in their brains for the right ones; they had the right ones in their mouths already. He wondered if you just got that way once you grew up. Probably not if you were Special Ed., you might never get that way.

The droolers. Room 19 was Special Ed., that was where the droolers were. He tried to remember seeing anyone drool in Room 19. He couldn't. In the classes when he was a little kid, some kids had drooled. But not in Room 19. Those chaperons maybe didn't know everything about Room 19. After all, they weren't in school. They had computers at their places and three stores. They probably knew everything about those things, just not everything about Room 19.

He looked through the tall windows. The dance floor was emptying. Girls in long dresses and guys with tuxedos were heading for the coatrooms.

The dance was over. Poor, poor Shana. She made her dress in that gloomy room. He couldn't figure it out.

Nick tried to find a place to wait for his father to pick him up, a place where everybody coming out of the dance wouldn't see him. It didn't work. There was no place like that. But he found that the darkness behind one of the columns in the place where he'd listened to the men talking was a little bit out of the way.

You couldn't say, Hi, how're ya doing? to people coming out of the prom, and he for sure didn't want any of them saying it to him.

He didn't have to wait long, maybe six minutes. His dad appeared in the car, and Nick ran fast toward it. A couple of kids tried to say hi to him, but he ran past them, scooting around long dresses. He jumped into the car fast, and slammed the door behind him.

His dad nearly jumped. "Hey, you still look pretty

good—the dancing didn't take much starch out. Where's Shana—getting her coat?"

How could you explain this bad thing? How can you explain something you don't know? He looked at the green dashboard lights.

Their car wasn't the only one leaving now, others were trying to get out of the parking lot. Some of the prom dancers had rented limousines, and the limousines were lined up, he could see five of them.

He was going to have to say something, and he was almost shaking cold by now. "Dad, could you turn the heat on?" he said.

"Sure." He moved the heat lever and the little red light went on. "Now I take you to the marina to get on the boat, right? Boy, what a night—I wish I were your age." His dad was smiling, not even tired-looking.

"No. Let's get out of here." He managed to say the words perfectly.

"Hey, what about—could we at least wait for Shana to get in the car?"

"No."

The turn of his father's neck looked angry. "What in the world—where are your manners, kid?"

"Shana couldn't come." There. He'd said it.

"What do you mean, she couldn't come?"

Nick tried to swallow, and couldn't. "She couldn't come to the prom." He looked at his knees and listened to the sound he didn't want to hear. It was the sound of his father moving around in the driver's seat, confused.

"Nick, tell me straight. You're saying Shana didn't come to the prom at all? Or she had to leave early? Or what?"

Nick felt terribly sorry for his father, having to ask those questions.

"She couldn't come, that's all."

"What happened? This afternoon she was—you said she—"

"I don't know, I don't know, I don't know. That's all."

His father breathed hard and played with the dashboard knobs.

"Nick, are you saying—" Nick looked at his father, his father looked at him, and there was an awful silence, and his father's face was lit by the headlights of other cars and by the green dashboard lights, and no words could come out, and in the silence a car honked, trying to get by. His father drove out onto the street. Nick heard him say something under his breath. Then he turned on the car radio and some kind of symphony played all the way home. Nick wanted to ask Dianne what he was supposed to do now.

When they got into the garage, his father asked him some more questions. You mean you waited for her and she didn't come to the dance? Did you go inside and dance? Did you go inside and have any refreshments? Are you cold?

None of the answers made any sense, so Nick didn't give any; he just said, Yes, he was cold.

They went into the house. Nick's mother wanted to know all about the prom, and where Shana was, and had they just come here to wash up before going on the boat ride, and . . .

His father started to explain. "No, listen, there's no boat ride tonight, uh, I mean, Nick isn't going on the boat ride—"

Then he turned toward Nick. "Listen, son, want to go on the boat ride anyway?" He looked hopeful, suddenly putting on happiness.

"No. I'm going to bed," Nick said.

"Nick, honey, what *happened*?" His mother would want the whole story, his father would, too. Nick didn't even know the whole story. How could he tell them? He was tired. No parents were going to be any good now, he just wanted to sleep.

He went up the stairs. Patsy leaped ahead of him.

His parents were whispering together. He could feel them standing in the living room, feeling sorry for him. If his mother started that "Oh, Nick, I love you so much" stuff, he was going to do something awful, he didn't know what.

He wished the fancy tuxedo and the cummerbund would disappear back to the Hindus, he wished he would disappear.

How in the world could anybody be such a jerk, such a drooler?

He tossed the tuxedo, section by section, on the chair by his desk. Most of it fell on the floor. Patsy jumped up on his bed and turned around and around, the way she always did, as if she was making a nest.

Jerk.

Drooler.

Maybe they didn't have car trouble.

When words leave your brain, you go to sleep.

5

In the nasty sunshiny morning, Nick kicked the heap of tuxedo and worked on Tree Frogs, but it wasn't really work, because he knew most of the North American ones already. He also didn't bother with frog stages. Didn't he raise two frogs by himself from egg chains in the pond three years ago? Yes.

His father came into his room, and Patsy came right along. She'd only been gone long enough to run outside for a few minutes. She put three paws on the amphibian chart, one of them right smack on the Squirrel Tree Frog, which sometimes huddles in groups of about twelve and lives on the Gulf Coast.

His dad stood in the doorway and looked down at Nick and Patsy and the amphibian chart. "Listen, son, you're gonna be really mad about what I did, so let's get that over with first. I made a phone call, I mean your mom and I made a phone call, and we talked to Shana's mother. Now, get mad and let's get that over with."

Mad wasn't the word. There wasn't any word. Nick looked at the Chorus Frogs.

What do you say to your father now? Do you just sit there on the floor in your pajamas with your dog slobbering on your shoulder?

Yes, that's what you do. And you hope you move out of this disgusting house when you're old enough. He looked up at his father. There was no word to say how disgusting this was.

His dad squatted on the floor on the other side of the amphibian chart. "Your mom and I love you very dearly. I can see you're angry. I would be, too. That's okay, son."

More disgusting yet.

"Get out of here." That was all Nick could think of to say.

"No. I'm not gonna get out of here yet. First I'm gonna tell you what Shana's mother said, and you're gonna listen, and then we're gonna talk about it, and *then* I'm gonna get out of here. Fair?"

No. Not fair. Being even more unfair, his dad sat all the way down on the floor, his feet in sneakers spread to two corners of the amphibian chart. Nick looked at him. Patsy lay down on the chart and hung her tongue out, drooling on the dorsolateral fold of the White-lipped Frog, who lays eggs in foam and lives in Mexico.

Nick looked at Patsy, then back at his father. It was disgusting.

"You took the corsage to Shana's house on your bike, right?"

Yes. Yes. Yes. Nick wanted to stick his tongue out at his father, but you couldn't do that, it was too childish. He didn't do anything.

"Is that right, Nick?"

This man could drive you crazy. "Yes." Period.

"Her mother put it in the refrigerator, right?"

This was a disgusting conversation. "Right." Did his dad want to hear about the refrigerator you could see through, too, clear down to the celery?

"And then did you come home and call Shana and tell her you'd decided not to go to the prom, you didn't feel well, or something like that?" His father's eyes were wide and asking the question, along with his mouth.

"No." Why would he do that?

"Then Shana made up a lie and that's what she told her mother. She said you'd decided—"

His father was stuck for finishing the sentence. Nick knew words for the end of the sentence, but they were terrible words, all of them. He could finish the sentence and make his father fall over backward, but he didn't. He put his hand on Patsy's head.

"Then you didn't call her and say—"

"No, I didn't pick up the phone, I came home and—" The rest of it was ridiculous: practicing dancing in front of the mirror, shaving twice, brushing his teeth four times, even practicing smiling. How ridiculous could you get, admitting that you practiced smiling?

"Shana got cold feet, I guess." His father looked awful. "She got to feeling funny about going to the prom. . . ." His voice faded out. "You know what I think, Nick? I think Shana got scared about going to the prom, I think she decided it would be easier not to go."

Easier not to go. Easier not to go to gym class, when you couldn't shoot even three baskets out of ten. Easier not to go to assemblies at school, when everybody knew you were a drooler. Easier, harder. Harder, easier.

"Listen: Her mother said you'd called, and you told Shana you didn't feel well and she could keep the corsage but you couldn't go to the prom. You mean none of that's true?"

"I told you, no. Now, get out of here."

His father didn't move. He just sat there on the floor, staring at the amphibians, upside down from where he sat. Now, his mother was standing in the doorway. A family party, with the dog and everybody. Now his mother would do her talking, and then they might leave him alone.

"Nick, if there were *any way* this might not've happened . . ." she said.

"I don't want to talk about it."

His mother got that miserable, hurt look on her face, and both parents left the room. Patsy stayed. That was exactly the way Nick wanted it. He couldn't imagine anybody he wanted to see but Patsy. Unless it was Dianne. Maybe Dianne could explain how anybody could be such a drooler. He stroked Patsy's big back and told her it wasn't her fault she was stuck with a drooler.

Not more than fifteen minutes later, his mother came to his room again, with his dad right behind her. Didn't they have anything else to do today but feel sorry for him? They could go to church or something, they usually went to Trinity Episcopal, where they kept hoping he'd get interested in being an acolyte. Acolyte, phooey. Nick believed in God, because it was probably God or some other name that thought up the planets and tides and the way things would evolve—probably it was some kind of god. But there were Hindus and Islams and Jews and some others and they might be true, too, so how could you carry a cross around in church and swear that was the only true story? It might be a Buddha God, and then the acolytes would be all wrong.

His parents should have gone to church.

"If it makes you feel any better, Shana's been grounded, her parents are furious," his mother said. She had everything turned around completely.

"I don't care."

She let her breath out hard. "Do you care about having waffles?"

"No."

His father looked up from staring at the Yosemite Toad, who lives in the high country and isn't a nocturnal toad. "What do you care about, Nick?"

"Nothing."

Another silence. "Son, believe me, you'll get over this, it just takes time. . . . You'll feel better . . ."

If his parents didn't get out of his room pretty soon, he was going to scream at them. "Just get out of here," he said in his normal voice.

That got rid of them. Nick shoved Patsy off the amphibian chart and she moved over beside his bed, her chin flat on the rug.

Shana didn't want to go to the prom with him. She said she did, but. There was nothing to go after the "but." But nothing. No reason he could figure out. Sure, he had zits. Two of them today, not very big ones, and one of them was on his neck, where you couldn't see it very much.

Because she'd gone Up. Going Up must be very fancy

if it means you can just decide not to go to the prom with your date.

Never, never, never did Nick want to go Up. In fact, he didn't want to go anywhere: not sideways or down or anything. He wouldn't go anywhere. That was a good decision.

It was because he was Special Ed. Shana was regular now, she must think Special Ed. was full of dummies and jerks and droolers.

Maybe she was right.

He stayed in his pajamas all day. What was there to get dressed for?

"Listen, Nick, you have to do something. If you don't want to watch the *National Geographic* special, you can at least eat dinner. Won't you eat dinner?" Blah blah blah.

Sometimes, if you knew a bad dream was coming, you could try to stay outside it, but you always lost. It was like going downhill on skis and having the snow fall out from under you. Usually you didn't know you were having a bad dream until you were in it. Then you could try to get outside it, but they kept you waiting just another minute longer before they let you out, and then they never let you out at all. You kept thinking, If I just wait one more little minute I'll be outside and then this bad thing won't happen, but you were always wrong.

Afterward, you woke up hating things and feeling terrible.

Maybe Bruce was right—if you dreamed in color, you were crazy. There were hot dogs on the grill, and there was the Pepsi right over there in the cooler. You went to get the Pepsi because you knew where it was, but you never got there.

You were walking on the white edges of the place, it was in the back of their house, but they wouldn't let you remember the names of the people. Mr. and Mrs. Something, but they took the names away from you in the sunshine. The trees were really tall, you couldn't see any town or street between them, just dark places where there were cedar smells and sometimes a Pepsi can in the dark at the edge of the daylight.

Mommy and Daddy were on the lawn, Mommy was lying on a long chair on the lawn, and she had the Band-Aid on her knee, and Daddy had his hand on the Band-Aid, and they were laughing with some other grown-ups, and it was boring, they had their bathing suits on but they didn't go swimming yet, Nick and Dianne pulled at Daddy's legs, each on one side, and Daddy laughed, Mommy said, Young ponies.

The morning was the ponies and they had rides, but in this dream they wouldn't let you on the rides, it was afternoon. Nick remembered the ponies, his pony had a blue saddle blanket, Dianne's pony had a green saddle blanket, and they ran fast but they wouldn't let you into that part of the dream, they didn't have time, it was a hurry.

When you wanted to go back to the ponies and the running in the field, they took you to the afternoon, after the ponies.

Nick looked at his legs below the bathing suit line, there were brown hairs from the pony, and Dianne was laughing. She was picking the gray pony hairs off her legs and she was laughing, and her red braids hung down her legs when she bent over to pick the pony hairs off and drop them on the ground.

The other children wanted to drink Pepsi, and some of them had orange juice, and they wanted to sit on the lawn with the grown-ups, and Dianne was running.

In a minute. In a minute. Nick heard the grown-up voices. In a minute.

Around the dark, cool shade of the house was the white edge of the place, and it was the deep part of the swimming pool. You were walking, slowly, because the white part was hurting on your feet, with little pebbles but they were glued down, you couldn't pick up the little pebbles, he knew because he tried.

Dianne laughed at him, he bent down to try to pick the pebbles out of the white edge of the swimming pool. Her bathing suit was blue and white with straps, he couldn't see the color of his, he was working at the pebbles with his fingers, squatting down on the white part of the edge.

There was wind in the cedar trees, just a little wind, and on the blue water there was just a little wind, too, just little ripples. He picked at the little pebbles in the white part between his feet, and Dianne ran right past him, with her running making a very little breeze on his back, and she jumped in the deep end.

He stayed squatting watching her, she was a girl with red braids jumping in the water, he saw the splash, and she came up. "This is how you tread water," she said. He wanted to tread water, and he watched her arms move, and her legs.

Now he would be able to tread water, but first he wanted his feet not to hurt on the pebbles, and he stayed squatting, picking at them, they wouldn't come up out of the white part you walked on.

Dianne spurted water out of her mouth, making parts

of circles with the drops coming out of her mouth and up and the drops falling down again into the water, and he could see her arms and legs move in the water and her blue and white straps and her shoulders.

"Hey, Daddy, we're going swimming," he said, and his voice couldn't get loud, they held it back so it was soft, but he tried it again, and the words wouldn't come out, they had a rule you had to be quiet now in your dream.

He wanted to be outside the dream now, and they wouldn't let him go anywhere, they made his legs heavy so he couldn't move, and he watched Dianne treading water, he watched her head go under, that was swimming.

Now he wanted to go outside the dream, and they held him there, and they made his voice slow down when he called DAAAAAAAAAAAADDDDDDDDDDDYYY, they wouldn't let him call faster, they slowed his throat, and now he still could call while Dianne was under the water swimming on the bottom of the deep end, DADDY, but they wanted him not to make noise, so they slowed him down again, and this time they held his legs.

Now Dianne should come up with her arms, you could move around in water, you could move sideways or any way. Nick saw her move sideways, and now he wanted to get out of the dream again, but they pushed his eyes this time, into the bottom of the pool, and there was a swirl of blue and braids, and now Daddy would get him out of the dream, he called again, but this time they held his voice and his legs and his arms and everything, and he heard his own voice not sounding.

He saw Dianne's bubbles, and he must get out of the dream, but they made him squat still, but he stood up and called Daddy and Mommy and there was the little wind over the top of the water and her bubbles, and she was moving her arms and legs on the bottom of the swimming pool, she was so excited now, swimming on the bottom of the pool, and now his eyes hurt and he was calling again, but they made him stop calling because Dianne was stopping the bubbles and he had to watch, that was the rule.

Now he had to get out of the dream, but they made him stay, and then they made him wait a long time, and he tried to run to the other side of the house, but they slowed him down with his feet inside the ground, and he was going as fast as he could, but that was very slow, and they wouldn't let him out of the dream.

And then everything got fast, his father and mother and everybody else running, and they all knew what to do but Nick didn't know, and he pointed with his arm to the pool and two men jumped into the pool and everyone was shouting and making a lot of noise and then Daddy was blowing in Dianne's mouth and pushing her shoulders on the white pebbly edge of the pool and she stayed still and now they still made you stay in the dream, it was your job to stay inside the dream with the wind blowing very cold and Dianne's blue and white bathing suit lying on the white edge of the pool with her tummy inside it not moving and her red braids lay on the white hard pebbly edge of the pool with the sun going down behind the cedar trees and her braids dripped on the white pebbly place, dropping water way off to the side of her tummy, and Nick would be willing to push her tummy to make it move but Daddy said No, in a long voice, and the wind blew cold on Nick's shoulders and he watched Dianne's tummy lying still and the wind blew again a little bit, and everyone was very cold, and it was quiet now, and they wouldn't let him out of the dream. They made him watch her eyes lying open, and her bottom had an accident on the white edge of the pool, and then Nick pulled on one of her braids and tried to yell at her to wake up and they wouldn't let him yell at her, and Nick was angry and he hit her tummy hard, two times and then again, with his hands, yelling her name and hitting her, and someone pulled his hands away from her tummy and held them tight and said Listen, Nick, it's no use, and he fought with the person's arms, men's arms, and he bit one arm and the arms let go and he hit Dianne again on her tummy and he yelled at her mouth and some-one put a hand over his yelling mouth and still he yelled her name and they wouldn't let him yell again and they finally let him out of the dream, and he felt the sheets on his bed and he looked at the clock beside his bed and he knew he was a failure, and then morning came when they wouldn't let morning come before, and he hated them. They were so unfair.

6

Waking up from the dream was almost as bad as being in it. The last time he had it was a long time ago, maybe about Thanksgiving. What was he supposed to do—thank them for not making him have it every single night?

He said again what he always said when he woke up from it: I'm sorry, Dianne. I'm sorry I hit your stomach so hard. I didn't know you were dead. I was trying to help.

Maybe he wasn't sorry enough? Maybe that was why they kept putting him into the dream over and over again— to make sure he was really good and sorry? How sorry was he supposed to get? You can't get any sorrier than I am, he said to the wall. I don't think there is any sorrier to get. I can't get any sorrier.

He should have run to get his parents the minute she jumped in the pool, he knew it, he knew it, he knew it. They make you go over the whole thing again and again so you'll never ever forget how wrong you were not to run to the other side of the house and get your parents soon enough. Dear God, I *know* how wrong I was.

Maybe if he wasn't Special Ed. he would have run all the way around the house in time. He didn't know he was Special Ed.

His parents told him later. They didn't know before, they said.

Fourth grade: Why can't I go to school in the room with Roger and Anthony? Because you have a little learning problem.

And he kept asking, first Mommy, then Daddy: What do you mean, I have a little learning problem?

That was when they got weird. They didn't know, they kept telling him. And he kept going into rooms and putting blocks together for a teacher, and then going into different rooms and telling another teacher what the pictures meant. Then he was supposed to read the story to the teacher, it was about the man and the fan and the frog and the dog. And there was the room where people put strange things on his head, they didn't hurt but they were strange. After all that, they still didn't know. He was just Special Ed., that was all.

After a while, Roger and Anthony didn't matter so much. Roger's parents got a divorce and he went to a different school, and Anthony moved away.

The bad dream always left him with a terrible day to look forward to. He couldn't stand breakfast, and he hated whatever he had to do that day. The day was something you learned to live through, but at least you knew you wouldn't have the same dream again the next night. You never had to have it two nights in a row.

And you couldn't talk about it to anybody. One time he'd tried, and his parents got disgusting. His mother cried and his father started saying it was nobody's fault, and then his mother joined in saying the same thing, but she did it crying, and then his father and mother both kept telling him how much they loved him and how much they loved each other, and pretty soon you couldn't hear yourself think because they were telling him over and over how wonderful he was, their wonderful son. It made you sick.

And then he remembered the prom.

Now: Does that make you a double failure? Or just one and a half failures, because once it was Dianne and she was your sister and she ended up dead, and this time it was just a girl who went Up and played a dirty trick?

Nick went through the motions of getting ready for school, but he knew he wasn't going. He wasn't going anywhere. His parents would get even worse if they knew, so he pretended.

The minute his dad's car drove out of the driveway, taking his dad to people's rotten teeth and his mother to Free Lunch, he could stop pretending.

His excuse was a real one: You couldn't go to school right after the dream about Dianne. Nobody should have to go to school right after the dream about Dianne. Nobody should have to go to school after that dream. And also, Shana would be at school, so he wouldn't be there. That was very simple. He couldn't talk about it to anybody, but it was very simple.

"Have a good day, dear."

"Thanks."

"Nobody's life is a bed of roses."

"Right."

"You're starting your project today, right?"

"Yep."

"Only six more weeks of school, then vacation. That'll cheer you up."

"Right."

It was amazing how you could fool your parents. Sometimes they just plain asked for it.

His parents drove away in the car, and Nick went back to bed. That dream was worse than running five miles for making you tired. He knew: He ran five miles last year to help Room 19 and other Special Ed. classes in Portland raise money for epilepsy or blindness or something. He was tired after that, but nothing like this.

He woke up at about noon.

In a movie sometime last year, a man's girlfriend said she wouldn't marry him after all, and he went home and started drinking whiskey, and pretty soon he felt better. After he drank some whiskey he started yelling at the television set, "I'm king of the everlovin' *world*," and he kept saying it. It was kind of funny. Nick went to the liquor cabinet, partly to see if it would work.

He found the whiskey bottle, he got a glass out of the cabinet, and he put some whiskey in it. It tasted terrible, but ice would make it better, so he put some ice in it. He turned the television set on. He watched some quiz shows and a show where everybody had something sad going on in doctors' offices and in restaurants. While he watched, he drank some more whiskey, counting the drinks. Patsy sort of watched TV with him.

The whiskey really did taste ugly, it burned his throat,

75

and pretty soon he was sleepy. He didn't feel like king of the world or anything, but he felt better. The television commercials were funnier than they usually were, and that was something.

By a little after four o'clock, he decided to take another nap. He'd had four glasses of whiskey and ice, and he hadn't spilled any. He hid the glass in the liquor cabinet. But he couldn't find the right knob on the television set right away, and that was funny, usually he knew all the knobs.

He had to make three tries at getting to the stairs to go to his room. That was funny, too. The stairs were more to his right than they used to be. "Hey, stairs, get back where you belong," he said, and laughed. Nick's Magic Moving Stairs.

He got to his bedroom and remembered the hair he'd found on his sweater. Shana's long, blonde, bendy hair. It was still on his desk, making a mess of things. Clean up your desk, Swansen, he said to himself. He found some matches and held one to the hair over the wastebasket, and watched it crinkle up and disappear.

He hit the bed on the second try. "Hi, bed," he said, and that was funny, too. His old friend the bed.

Then it was the ceiling that started to move. He closed his eyes and had to hang onto the bed to keep the ceiling in place. It was worse with his eyes closed, so he opened them, and then that seemed worse. Patsy was walking around, it made him dizzy to watch her. He decided to stare at one corner of the room, and that was the last thing he remembered.

He was sick to his stomach, and he woke up. He tried

to make it to the bathroom, but his stomach beat him in the race. He was only partway out of the door of his bedroom when he threw up.

He couldn't stop throwing up, and then he couldn't throw up enough. Please don't let Mom and Dad get home now, he said to the floor.

He got the mop, and the bucket, and the smelly cleaning stuff from the kitchen, and he put the stuff in the bucket and put some water with it, and he mopped, and Patsy kept getting in his way, and then he knew he needed a sponge to get the corners near the door, and the bottom part of the door, so he used a sponge from the bathroom, and he scrubbed and he scrubbed, and then he had to throw up again, but this time the bucket was right in front of him, and so now he had a mess on the floor, and a mess in the bucket, and he had a monster of a headache. Patsy walked away. Smart dog.

Not king of the everlovin' world at all.

Jerk. Moron. Double triple stupid jerk.

And he had to hurry so his parents wouldn't get home too soon and find out.

Not only the mess on the floor and the door and part of the rug, but on his shirt, too. After the bucket and mop and sponge, he had to rinse his shirt in the bathtub and hang it up on the shower nozzle before he went back to bed. King of the everlovin' world, ha.

My head, my triple bad head, was the last thing he remembered before he went to sleep again.

He said no to dinner and kept sleeping, off and on. He heard his parents, outside his room, talking about pressure and tension and stress and how difficult this must be for him, and he let them talk. When it got dark, Patsy came in and climbed up on his bed, turning around and then settling down to sleep.

The Larch Mountain Salamander was walking over pieces of rotten wood, calm in the mossy Douglas fir, just a few miles away. It had a nice life, living soft along the ground. Not causing trouble, just looking around and going along, breeding and maybe even evolving some more. Just being there, in its right place, doing its work of living.

Nick woke exhausted, and knew it was Tuesday. Tuesday morning.

By 7:10, his mother was at his door, knocking. Knocking nicely, but still, any kind of knocking was knocking, and it interrupted things, no matter what things they were. These things were just thoughts about the two men outside the prom, with computers and three stores where you could probably have anything you wanted free, if you owned them. But they were thoughts, anyway, and his mother interrupted them.

"Hi, sweetheart, you feeling better this morning?"

"No." Nick was propped up in bed, with two pillows behind him, staring at the door as it opened. His mother was going to be worried now, and she'd do that stuff about how she wanted to be a good mother and all the rest of it. Maybe he should have said, yes, he did feel better. Patsy jumped off his bed and went out the door.

"Listen, dear, I know it's not a fever, but will you jump all over me if I just feel your forehead?" Mothers had this thing for fevers; they had a thing for either sticking a hand on your forehead or a thermometer in your mouth. Most of the people in Room 19 had mothers who did it, too, they discussed it one day when Mr. Norton got interested in why Becky wasn't in school for several days, they talked about mothers and their hand always on your forehead or looking for a thermometer. Mr. Norton thought it was funny. He said he never knew till now that his mother was like all the other mothers in America, or maybe he said all the mothers in North America, and he laughed really hard, but nobody else did. He said he thought his Room 19 kids just didn't look hard enough for funny things about mothers, and they should know now that this thing about them was funny. He poked his hands in the air with all of his fingers straight out and laughed and laughed, and still nobody else laughed. He called them spoilsports.

Suddenly now, Nick laughed. Mr. Norton's mother and Becky's mother and everbody else's mother, all with one hand on your forehead and the other hand reaching like something in a cartoon, outside your room, way down the hall to the bathroom, finding a thermometer without even looking, just feeling around and finding one, and yanking the stretching hand back into your room, shaking out the thermometer as it came.

"Hey, you're laughing. That's a good sign. So, you'll go to school. That's great." She'd walked into his room, smiling, picking up three socks and hanging onto them as she walked.

"No."

"What do you mean, no? It's a perfectly gorgeous day, we've all got lots to do, you've got lots to learn today—"

"No." He was getting more sure, the more his mother talked. He wouldn't go. He would not go.

She started her frown. "Why not, Nick?" She stood at the foot of his bed and asked him. There was no answer. He looked at the wall, with its paint chipped away from having posters taped to it once. He used to have a *Star Wars* poster on that wall. Now the yellow paint was chipped off in four places where the poster tape used to be.

"I'm not going to school." That was all.

Suddenly she had her hand on his forehead, and it wasn't funny anymore. It had been funny in the thought of it, but now that she had her hand there it wasn't funny at all.

"It's a bad day. I'm having a bad day," he said. That would take care of it. You couldn't tell someone wasn't having a bad day from having your hand on his forehead. Of course, having a bad day was true, but it wasn't anything he could even begin to explain. Where would he start?

After all, Dianne must be even worse for his mom. Even worse, if you had your own baby out of your own body and she drowned one day—

She took her hand away from his head and hugged him. "Hugs are good for you when you're having a bad day," she said into his ear. She hugged him tight, still holding the three socks. The best you could do was just let her hug you and wait till she finished.

"You want French toast, then?" She straightened up and seemed happier. "You didn't have dinner last night, you must be hungry. French toast?" She was getting all excited about making it, you could tell.

"No."

She put her hand on his arm, sticking out of the covers. "Are you sure, dear?"

"No. Yes. I'm sure."

He knew she was starting to cry when she went out the door, you could always tell from behind. And she forgot to put the three socks in the laundry hamper as she went.

"I'll see you at five o'clock, I'm riding to work with Dad again today. Call me if you want to," she said, with her head held high and stiff.

"Okay."

A few minutes later she was outside the door again, knocking and asking, "Shall I send Patsy back in, then?"

That one he could answer, no problem. "Sure."

The door opened, and in she came, the good old girl dog. Sometimes when he felt awful he reminded Patsy that he'd saved her from the pound. Up she jumped onto his bed now. She stuck her black front foot on his right leg and her white front foot on the covers between his legs, and she laid her three-colored face on his stomach. She must weigh almost seventy pounds now, and she was about six years old. When you got a dog from the pound you never knew exactly how old it was.

And then he felt horrible: All those other dogs in the pound with Patsy never got families, they never got saved. You couldn't take them all, and you ended up taking one and being happy that you had Patsy and guilty about the others. They all looked nice, too, when you looked at them. Every single one of them needed a family or they'd end up dead.

He'd sent more than twenty or thirty dogs to the gas chamber when he wasn't even ten years old yet.

You couldn't be called a baby if you cried because you'd done something really horrible. Not really. He thought about the other dogs in the pound, ones with tall ears, ones with eyes that didn't match, ones with waggly heads, and ones with heads that stood still and stared at your eyes. He chose Patsy because she had so many colors.

He didn't know really why else he chose her; he was a little kid.

And he was a criminal.

Patsy moved on his bed and marched up to lick his face. He wanted to hate her for being saved when the other dogs got sent to the gas chamber, and there she was, licking his tears.

Guilty murderer, that's what he was. But probably some of them got families later. And probably lots of them didn't. PROBABLY: that nasty word again. Probably everything in the world. PROBABLY could really make you go batty and lose your brain.

He wanted to scream.

This time it was his dad at his bedroom door. "Nick, is Patsy in there?"

You could fake not crying. "Yeah." If you kept to very few words, or maybe just one.

"Can I come in and say good-bye to both of you?"

"Yeah." You couldn't say no, there was no way you could say no when your dad asked that kind of question. He ran his right pajama sleeve across his nostrils fast.

The door opened. He looked at his dad, all dressed to be a dentist for the day, coming across the room not looking at the clothes on the floor. Mothers couldn't walk across a room that way, and fathers usually did, Nick decided. But that was a probably, too.

"Which is the dog and which is my son?" his dad laughed, patting Patsy's back. "Oh, that's right—the dog is the one with the big wet tongue. You and Pats going to have a busy day? What've you got planned, son?"

Nick thought about the way his dad had looked late Saturday night, saying No, No, No to him.

I look stupid in a tuxedo. No, No, No. I'm a fool and a jerk. No, No, No. All the way upstairs to his bedroom, No, No, No. Then Nick had slammed the door, and his father was still standing at the foot of the stairs saying No, No, No.

"I'm gonna do amphibians," Nick said. He didn't say it right, the m's came out like crying, sounding like b's.

"Move, Patsy." His dad pushed the dog over and sat down on the side of the bed. "I love you, Nick," he said.

Nick looked at the chipped yellow paint on the wall.

His dad pounded him lightly on the shoulder with his fist, making a little tiny sound on his pajamas. "Life ain't easy, son," he said. He might start My Gramps told me life ain't easy, and he might not.

Nick had sent lots of dogs to the gas chamber when he was a kid, just to have Patsy, and now his dad was saying life ain't easy. Parents are impossible, they can be so dense. He couldn't look at his father.

"Call me at work if you get bored, okay?"

Now he was supposed to spend the day calling his parents at work. Dense, dense, dense. He just wanted his dad to go away.

"I've gotta go now, son. You want anything?" His dad stood up.

"No."

"Okay, you work on cheering up, along with the amphibians."

"Take Patsy with you, okay?"

"Very funny, a dog in the waiting room."

That wasn't funny. "I mean take her out of here and shut the door."

His dad shrugged his shoulders and took the dog and closed the door.

No school. No parents. What would he do?

He listened to Patsy whining outside his bedroom door, he listened to the garage door opening and the starting of a car.

"Yes!" he shouted. "Yes! I want French toast, Mom!"

He listened to the sound of a car driving away, then he listened to no sound at all.

7

By Wednesday morning, Nick was listing things in the week. Monday, got drunk and threw up. Tuesday, made French toast and it burned so Patsy ate it. Also Tuesday, Mom and Dad almost yelled at each other. You're too gentle with him, no, *you're* too gentle with him, listen, we're all in this together, it's nobody's fault, that's right, it's really nobody's *fault*, well, when is he going back to school, you can't just wait till you *feel* like going back to school, I know, I know, he's having a hard time and I don't blame him, I don't *blame* him either, we have to *do something*. . . .

It wasn't really yelling but they were getting close.

Wednesday, work on amphibians.

And he did. He decided to have a whole section of his project for just Oregon species. The Oregon Salamander, and the Oregon Slender Sal, its underside is the opposite of the Oregon. The Oregon has tiny black speckling on white or pale yellow, and the Oregon Slender has large white spots on its black belly. And of course, he'd have the Larch Mountain.

And he ate the tuna fish sandwiches that were left in the refrigerator for him when he wanted to eat them, instead of when the bell rang at 11:57 for first lunch.

It was a warm day in May, and everyone else was in school, and he was walking around his bedroom in bare feet. If he went to school, Shana would be there. He'd be a jerk and a drooler. Everybody would know what Shana did about the prom.

Everybody would be working on their end-of-year projects. Somebody always did Things You Can Learn from TV, and somebody always did The Elephants at Washington Park Zoo. The elephants were famous. And usually somebody did the Explosion of Mt. St. Helens. The two Down's syndrome ones didn't have to do their projects in writing, they could just answer questions about How to Wash Dishes or What You Do on a Camping Trip or How to Take Care of Your Pet.

Some people had a hard time choosing a project, but Nick never did. Last year he did Dirt. He used a square foot of dirt three inches deep that he dug from behind the football field, and he identified everything he could find in it. That was why Mr. Norton said he should go in Tuesday science this year, Mr. Wakamatsu thought his dirt project was so good.

Last year Shana did How a Sewing Machine Works, and she drew diagrams and explained everything, and she pasted pieces of material on the pages with stitches on them, showing what happens when the thread gets tangled in the machine and what happens when it goes right. Her project was the best in the class.

Shana and her sewing machine.

Room 19 drooler Swansen.

He was trying to figure out how to say "ambystomatidae," the Mole Salamanders with teeth going across the roofs of their mouths, when a screech of tires and a yelping interrupted him. The voice of a hurt dog always sent a knifing pain down his backbone. A neighbor's dog, maybe the gold one, or the Airedale next door. It wouldn't be Patsy, she was in the living room or somewhere. He ran outside to look.

Just past the end of the driveway Patsy lay on her side in the sunshine, her tongue hanging out, her left hind leg in a bad position. Nick ran. He knelt down on the street beside her and felt the leg, and she lurched her head so fast he didn't even see her bite his left arm. It hurt like crazy even before it started to bleed.

He heard the breath push out of his mouth hard. But you had to keep a dog still, you couldn't let it get up and try to walk if it had a broken bone or something. He wouldn't touch that leg again, and Dr. Samuels would know what to do. He looked at the blood coming out of his arm, halfway between his elbow and his wrist, and he wiped it on his jeans and said, "You'll be okay, Patsy."

The car had hit her and gone on, it wasn't anywhere. What kind of person would do that? Just up and drive away? He stroked Patsy's head and thought about what to do. The vet's office was too far to walk if he carried her. If he went to the neighbors' houses and told them he had to get his dog to Dr. Samuels, Patsy would get up and try to walk and ruin her leg. And besides, just about everybody was at work or school, so he couldn't do that. His arm hurt. He wiped the blood on his pants again.

"We'll go to the vet, Pats," he said, and when he said it he knew what he would do. He took off his T-shirt and tied it around Patsy's mouth. It was hard, he had to try four times. She kept moving her head.

He tried to explain. "I'm gonna put you in Mom's car. If I don't put this around your mouth, you'll bite me again, and I can't drive the car then. We're gonna go to the vet." He wiped the blood again and put both arms under her. He made sure to stay away from her hurt leg, and he took a deep breath and stood up.

Patsy was a heavy dog. But she wasn't fighting. "Good Patsy," he said, and he walked up the driveway to the garage. He could open the car door with one hand without moving his wrist against her. She was making angry noises under his T-shirt. He put her on the floor in front of the front seat. "I'm gonna leave your mouth tied up, we're gonna go to the vet, then you'll get untied." He closed the car door and ran to the kitchen to get the key out of the cupboard drawer, and he grabbed a towel to wrap around his arm. He ran back and got in the car. Then he wrapped the towel around his arm and tucked in the corners so it wouldn't come loose, and he turned the ignition key.

The car started just fine. A little bit noisy. And the car radio was playing music, he left the radio on. He strapped himself in, it was a state law to wear your seat belt.

"Patsy, I don't know how to drive a car," he said. But "R" was for reverse, and that's what you use to drive a car backwards, and he backed out of the garage. The driveway sloped a little bit and wasn't very long. They only went over three flowers, he could see them when they got to the street, and he pushed the brake and the engine stopped.

He tried to remember what his parents had told him. A car has a clutch. Right next to the brake. He pushed the clutch in and nothing happened. He took his foot off it. You've got four gears. Try first gear, push the shift toward the "1." He turned the key, and the car started and then stopped.

He looked at Patsy. The car started to roll, and he put his foot on the brake and turned the key at the same time, and it sounded right. "What did I do this time?" he asked Patsy. He looked at his foot on the pedal. It wasn't the brake, it was the clutch. He'd made a mistake, and the car was moving. He kept his foot on the clutch and went very slowly up the street. The music on the radio ended, and the man said he was going to play Beethoven next. Beethoven kept following Nick around.

At the stop sign he changed feet and put his foot on the brake, keeping the clutch pushed in. Then he changed his feet again, to use the gas pedal. There was no other traffic, just houses going by and the radio music.

They went another block. "We've gone two blocks," he said to Patsy. "We're going to the vet." They had to turn, and he used the turn signal the way it was in the driver's manual. He steered too far and came very close to a blue car that was parked, but they didn't hit. "I almost hit a car," he said to Patsy. Then they came to a traffic light, and it stayed green, and they went along. He concentrated on steering.

And then suddenly he couldn't see anything. A smear of blazing white light hit his eyes, and he kept his hands on the wheel and tried to steer, and the car stopped with a dull sound against the curb, and he heard a clattering of metal,

Berwick Public Library
P.O. Box 838
Berwick, ME 03901

like pots and pans being dropped. The engine stopped. Through the blobs of light in front of his eyes he could see that he'd steered the car crooked. The music stopped.

A policeman was standing beside the car, looking down at Nick through silvery sunglasses. "Kid with the mirror got you, did he? Can I see your license?" He had a mustache like two black toothbrushes.

"I couldn't see." Nick looked around. He'd knocked over a garbage can. It was rolling back and forth on the edge of the curb.

"It's the old mirror trick. My partner's gone to talk to the kid's mother, he'll be scared to do it again. Your license."

The garbage can stopped rolling. Nick said, "My dog got hit, I have to take her to the vet."

"Too bad. She bleeding or what? Can I see your license?"

"I don't think so."

"Don't push me, kid. I *said* your *license*." Like a cop in a movie.

"I don't have one." Now he might go to jail.

"You don't have a license, but you're driving your dog to the vet. Is that a very logical thing to do, son? Whose car is this?"

He had to explain. "My mother's. I'm Special Ed. I think my dog's leg is broke, a car hit her." It was too much to explain all at once.

"Well, Ed, we're going to park your mother's car right here and lock it up, and we're going to take your dog to the vet. Does your mother know you're driving her car?"

"No."

"That's theft, and driving without a license—come on, get out. Get in the back of the police car over there." The cop opened the door. "What happened to your arm, Ed? And where's your shirt?"

"My name is Nick, she bit me, I put my shirt—"

"And where are your shoes?" The policeman parked Nick's mother's car right in front of the police car, and Nick got into the backseat of the police car. The policeman asked, "This dog bite?"

Nick leaned out the window. "No," he said. "Well, she bit me but—"

"Well, you've got her muzzled, right?"

"What do you mean?"

The cop's mouth looked digusted. "Never mind," he said.

"It's her hind leg—her left one—"

The cop was lifting Patsy out. She growled under the T-shirt, but the policeman laid her gently in Nick's lap. Nick tried to explain to her. "Patsy, we're going to the vet, like I promised. You'll be okay."

Another policeman came, without sunglasses, both cops got in the front seat and slammed the doors. "Okay, Ed, where's the vet?" asked the one with the mustache.

Nick told him where Dr. Samuels's office was.

"We're gonna call your mother and tell her about the car. What's her name and where do we find her?"

Nick told him it was Free Lunch, and told him the phone number, and said his name was Nick. The other cop was writing it all down.

"What's your dog's name, Ed? How come you're not in school?" said the one who did all the talking. He must not have heard the part about Nick's name. The one doing the writing didn't say anything. Maybe he didn't hear.

Nick said her name was Patsy. "What got in my eyes?" he asked.

"I told you, it's the mirror trick. You hold a mirror to catch the sun and reflect it in people's eyes. This one's a real little kid. Too little to go to school, big enough to cause accidents. How come you're not in school?"

"I'm sick, I have a cold or something." Theft, and driving without a license, and lying. Nick looked at Patsy, and then closed his eyes.

The vet's nurse was the same one as always; she'd known Patsy from the very beginning. Nick showed her Patsy's leg by pointing his head to it. She looked at everybody and buzzed Dr. Samuels.

"Doctor, I have Patsy Swansen with an injured leg, and Nick Swansen half naked with a bloody arm wrapped in a dish towel, and two very nice policemen who want to use the phone, and I think you'll want to take a look at all of them." Dr. Samuels took Nick and Patsy into an examining room that had jars of worms in liquid on the counters.

Nick could hear the policeman with the mustache telling his mother on the phone that he had her son Ed with him and where her stolen car was parked and that her car key would be at the precinct. Nick tried to imagine his mother listening to him. She'd be thinking her car was stolen and she didn't have a son named Ed.

As soon as Nick put Patsy on the examining table, he knew how scared he was. She might have to be killed. They do that to dogs that can't get well. He put his hand on her head. He'd kept telling her she'd be all right. What if that was a lie? What kind of person were you if you lied to your own dog?

Dr. Samuels looked at Nick's T-shirt wrapped around Patsy's mouth and said, "Good work, Nick." He rolled both her eyelids back with his fingers and said, "Hmmm." He took some gauze out of a drawer and wound it around the T-shirt, twice, then he wrapped it around her neck. "We'll need this extra muzzle," he said.

That was what the cop meant, then. You've got her muzzled. Nick looked at Dr. Samuels's round face. He had round glasses and a round stomach, and big round arms.

Dr. Samuels put a stethoscope against Patsy's chest. He even had round ears. A hypodermic needle appeared. "I'll give her this cortisone first; she's not in severe shock, but this is to stabilize her blood pressure," he said. He gave the shot in her front leg. "Now, let's see what we've got."

He felt around on her left hind leg. Nick watched his hands. They were round, too. "Well, Nick, there's a fracture here. We'll X-ray to see just what it looks like, but it's a fracture. She'll rest tonight, and I'll do the surgery in the morning."

"Surgery?"

"She's probably going to get a pin in her leg."

Patsy lay on the table, staring at the jars of worms. Nick tried to think of a pin in her leg. "What kind of pin?" he asked.

"It's stainless steel, and we put it into the fractured femur. It goes into the marrow cavity, it gives the strength her broken bone hasn't got. Don't worry, Nick. We do quite a few of these."

She wasn't going to die. But maybe she was. He looked at the vet.

"You'll have your dog, Nick. Almost as good as new. We'll splint her. Dogs heal fast. Here, let me clean that arm. She bit you?" He unwrapped the towel and worked at the bite with a swab and something from a bottle. "You're the first human I've treated this week. This is just betadine, it's a disinfectant. Does the bite hurt?"

"A little. Is she gonna be able to walk?"

"She'll run, Nick. You know what they say: God made dogs to run on three legs, he just couldn't decide which three. How'd you get the police to bring you? Where are your shoes?"

Nick told him some of it while he watched his arm being bandaged. He left out the part about the cop calling him Ed. Dr. Samuels kept smiling. "When did you learn to drive, Nick?"

"I didn't." And he explained about keeping the clutch pushed in.

Dr. Samuels laughed. "Nick, you've done just about everything right except the clutch. You're a smart kid. Hey, wait—why aren't you in school? Out early today?"

"No." Nick looked at the jars of worms. No, he wasn't smart. No, he wasn't out early. No, he wasn't going to tell Dr. Samuels. He bent over Patsy on the table and put both arms around her neck.

"Hmmm. She can go home tomorrow or the next day. Give us a call in the afternoon, all right? How are you getting home?"

"I'll walk."

"In your bare feet? Here, take your towel. Patsy'll be fine."

Nick looked at her. She didn't know she was going to

have an operation. He picked up the bloody towel with one hand and put the other hand on her head. "Thanks," he said to Dr. Samuels.

"You're welcome, Nick. You did a good job. We'll put her together."

As Nick walked home, he looked at bumper stickers. Honk if you like beer. Something your local something. I'm not retarded, this car was a gift. Have you something your kid today? Teach peace. Ex-wife in trunk. Are we having fun yet? Christ is coming.

A sign in a pet shop window said, "All kittens 1/2 price." They must have something wrong with them.

Did he let Patsy out and forget her? Who hit her and drove away?

Those weren't the things his parents wanted to know. When Nick walked in the door, everybody was in the living room. His dad was standing at the big window that was really six little windows. Each window had a part of the big picture in it, but you could pretend to take one part away, and then somebody's roof or a part of a tree would disappear.

"How could you just get in the car and drive off without a license, Nick?" his father asked.

"I kept my foot on the clutch."

"You *what?*"

"I kept the clutch pushed in." Nick was sitting sideways on the arm of a big green chair. He and Dianne used to make a fort with that chair and three others and some blankets, in the other house. Once they ate cherry pie in the fort, and Dianne said not to tell Mommy. They sat with their backs leaning against the place where his ankles were right now and ate the cherry pie. Then they hid the plates under the chair for a long time, and Mommy never figured out who stole some of the pie.

Nick looked at his mother. What would happen if he told her about the cherry pie right now? She'd left work, picked up her car key, and gotten her car. She was sitting on the sofa with the key and her purse in her lap, and there was a head of cauliflower in a plastic bag beside her.

His father gave his mother an annoyed look, and then he turned around and walked across the living room, from the window to the piano. He plunked three notes and went back to the window. Looking out the window with his back to Nick, he said, "That's not what I meant. *How* could you just drive away when you knew you were breaking the law?" You could still hear the notes he'd played, as if they were stuck on the walls.

"Patsy was hurt."

"Why didn't you call me? I'd have come home," his mother said.

The answers to both his parents' questions were just about the same. He had to hurry to get Patsy to the doctor.

"But you don't have a license, Nick." His mother.

"He doesn't even have shoes or a shirt, evidently." His father. He was walking again, from the window to the piano. He hit more notes, lower this time. The sound stayed in the room again.

"Who let the dog out and forgot her?" Nick asked.

Nobody remembered who had let her out. "You could've had an accident." His mother.

"He did have an accident." His father. He walked from

the piano to the window again and ran his hand up and down the edge of the blue curtain. Jays were screeching at each other in the spruce tree.

"It was an accident anybody could have had." His mother.

"You hit something, that's technically an accident." His father.

"It was only a garbage can." His mother.

Then they started where they'd left off the night before. You're too gentle with him. *I'm* too gentle with him? It's really nobody's fault. No, it's really nobody's fault. You can't go around breaking laws. We have to do something. Yes, we have to do *some*thing.

Nobody mentioned Patsy. Nick tried to leave the living room, and then it was You'll stay right here, young man. . . .

He had to go to school the next day. "You have to, Nick. Enough is enough," his mother said, holding the cauliflower in her hands in its plastic bag. In science they tell you a brain is like a cauliflower. His dad was sitting on the piano bench now, with his back to the piano and his elbows on his knees and his hands hanging down.

"You're punishing me when some jerk hit Patsy and drove away?"

"Nobody's punishing anybody," said his dad. "School's where you belong, and Patsy's going to be all right, and you have work to do, and your mother and I have work to do, and you're lucky you didn't get killed—"

There was a fierce quiet in the living room. You could hear the lawn sprinkler ticking and a fly angry on the windowsill looking for a way out. Nick looked at his mother and dad. If he got killed, they wouldn't have any children left at all. Just two people staring at each other and hitting notes on the piano until they got so old they died.

When he was really little, his dad took him exploring. It was a hot day. You had to climb down a long bank to the creek, and your feet might slip, and you could fall in the sticker bushes. Nick was wearing short pants, and his leg got scratched once. The creek was foamy white and then plain dark and then foamy and then dark again. It made different sounds in different places, a foamy sound and a black sound and a sand sound. Where the sun was on the water, it hurt your eyes to stare at it. It had round stones like little elephants sleeping, and you could pick wild blackberries and wash them in the creek and eat them. You could build a dam with wet sand and keep the water in a pool, but you had to keep building up the walls or they'd wash away. They used thimbleberry leaves for rafts, and they tried to see how many alder cones they could float on a leaf raft. Daddy squatted on the edge of the sand with one foot on a round stone and floated a leaf with alder cones on it, and Nick ran downstream to catch the raft when it came near the shore. The thimbleberry leaves felt soft and velvety if you rubbed them one way and rough if you rubbed them the other way. Sometimes the rafts didn't come near the shore at all, they went on down the creek. After a while they traded places, and Nick floated the rafts for Daddy to catch. Daddy could reach far out into the creek to catch them.

It was shady when they were finished exploring. The bank was too steep for Nick to climb, and Daddy carried him on his back, holding his elbows under Nick's bare knees. Partway up the hill, they stopped and Daddy had a stick of Juicy Fruit gum and he broke it in half. He put half in Nick's mouth and he took the other half. He told Nick to duck his head so the sticker bushes wouldn't scratch him. He ducked his head against Daddy's dark blue, scratchy shirt and chewed the Juicy Fruit gum and rode all the way to the top of the bank, bouncing along on his father's back.

He looked across the living room at his father sitting on the piano bench, bent forward and staring at the rug. Nobody said anything.

"Well," his dad said, suddenly clapping his hands together and standing up, "who's gonna drive to the doctor and who's gonna cook dinner?"

"I'll cook, you drive," his mother said. She stood up and rolled the cauliflower around in her hands. She looked like somebody getting ready to shoot from the free throw line. They're always thinking when they do that.

"What do you mean, doctor?" Nick asked.

"Tetanus shot, remember? We have to be there in half an hour. Let's get moving," said his dad. "Put some shoes on, Nick."

"And a shirt." His mother.

"And comb your hair." His dad.

"Dr. Samuels put betadine on it," Nick said, getting up off the chair.

"He's a veterinarian," his dad said. He took keys out of his pocket.

"He's a veterinarian," his mother said, moving toward the kitchen.

Nick was almost at the top of the stairs when his mother almost shouted. "What's blood doing all over this towel?"

"I put it on my arm," he called. He heard her turning on water. He was tired of explaining things. He threw cold water on his face, combed his hair, found a T-shirt on a chair, and put on socks and sneakers.

His mother was in the dining room. She looked at him as he walked through. "Nick, why did the policeman think your name was Ed?"

Why couldn't he get a driver's license if he was sixteen? Why didn't Shana go to the prom? How could he walk into Room 19 tomorrow? Who hit Patsy and drove away?

You couldn't help feeling sorry for her, standing there in a green dress and holding a handful of knives and forks and napkins. It was as if she hoped she could make things start going right if she set the table—as if three people could sit down and eat dinner and then everything would be all right.

"Forget it, Mom," he said.

On the way to Dr. Willis's office, Nick watched his father's feet.

"It's tricky, you have to *feel* how fast to let the clutch out, and you learn that only by doing it, son," his dad said. "We're due for another driving lesson, aren't we?"

"Yeah," Nick said.

"How about Saturday afternoon? The parking lot at work?"

One week after he'd taken Shana her pink rosebud corsage on his bike, one week after he'd stood outside the hotel in a rented tuxedo and watched the prom. Patsy might be dead on the operating table. "Okay," he said.

"You don't sound very interested."

"Yeah, I want to." Nick sat up a little straighter. Fooling your parents was so easy it was ridiculous. All you had to do was fake being happy.

Dr. Willis wanted to clean out the bite again, and put another bandage on it. Nick thought maybe she'd take stitches, but she said no, she wouldn't stitch his arm because there might be bacteria inside. He'd have to take penicillin pills.

Dr. Willis—his dad called her Shirley, he went to school with her or something—had one straight eye and one eye that looked into the side of her nose. Sometimes you couldn't tell where she was looking. Nick wondered how she could do operations on people if she saw the side of her nose all the time. She wasn't ugly, but she had that sideways eye.

"How's school, Nick?" she asked. He could make up another lie and say it was fine. His dad was in the waiting room, he wouldn't hear him. How many lies could you tell in one day?

"I don't want to talk about it," he said. He looked at a photograph on the wall. It was somebody standing on snow, wearing goggles and a backpack. "Who's that in the"—he breathed in very fast while she put the tetanus needle in his arm—"picture?"

She took the needle out of his arm. "That's me. On top of Mt. Hood. Last summer. I'm going up Rainier next month. Mountain climbing bug's got me. I bought a new ice axe and have to try it out."

"You went all the way to the top?" She was putting something on his arm. It smelled and felt and looked exactly like betadine. "What're you putting on my arm?"

101

"It's betadine. Yes, all the way. And I felt it for the next three days. Why don't you want to talk about school, Nick?" He shut his eyes and tried to think about being on top of a mountain.

"You're hurting, aren't you?" she said.

He opened his eyes. "No, it's not bad."

"I don't mean your arm." She stopped working on his arm, and put her hand flat on his chest, right up against his heart. "I mean right there. Am I right?" She took her hand away and went on with the betadine.

He looked down at his pants leg. There was blood on it, dried to brown. Patsy's leg must hurt terribly. Where would she be now?

"I'm okay," he said. Another lie.

Dr. Willis started to put the bandage on. "I'm going to tell you something, Nick. Nobody's completely okay. Think about it," she said.

"What do you mean?"

"Just think about it." She was still doing the bandage. "I mean, every single person in the world has something not okay. Something hurting. That's the way it is. Which means"—she started to put some tape on the bandage—"which means it's perfectly natural to hurt. Everybody's doing it. It's not fun, but it's necessary." She smoothed the tape with her hand. "Or, it seems to be. Now, I want you to keep this arm out of the shower for a few days. And I want to see you again on Monday. We're done for today. You going to think about what I said?" She wrote out a prescription for penicillin.

"Yeah." He just wanted to get out. "Thanks. For the bandage and stuff. And the shot."

"You're welcome, Nick. I love getting thanked for jabbing people."

On the way home he asked his dad about Dr. Willis's eye.

"She was born that way. She had surgery three times, but it didn't work."

"You went to school with her or something?"

"College. She was your mom's roommate."

Nick's arm hurt. He thought about Patsy.

"She wanted to be an astronaut."

"Mom?"

"No. Shirley. They wouldn't let her in the training program because of her eye. So she went to medical school instead. Everybody expected her to come out an eye doctor. But she decided to be a family doctor instead. How does your arm feel, son?"

"It's okay." That wasn't a lie. It hurt, but it was okay. "Who let Patsy out this morning?"

His father shook his head. "I don't know, Nick. Nobody remembers. Memory's a funny thing. Somebody did, that's all we know." They stopped at the drugstore to get the penicillin.

Nick's amphibian things were in his pack. He practiced "ambystomatidae" in bed, but he didn't know how to say it. Even if he could say it and spell it and tell everybody in the whole school what it meant, he'd still be a drooler in Room 19. Shana was going to be in school. She'd be laughing with her new friends and swinging her long hair down the hall. Bruce and Jason Bartholomew were smart enough not even to try to go to a prom, he was dumb enough to try to. Ambymat—Ambymost—Amsti—

Jerk. He was ten times a jerk.

What kind of world was God running, anyway? He turned the pillow over and bunched it up under his head.

In his dream, he was driving a car, but it wasn't his mother's. He had to go someplace, he was going to be late. He couldn't make the car go fast enough, he could get there faster if he walked. He saw people standing on the sidewalk laughing at him. It was a whole bunch of people laughing and pointing, but he didn't know any of them. Then he knew why they were laughing: The car had a bumper sticker that said "Room 19." He didn't know how he knew that, he was inside the car and couldn't see the bumper. And there was a cauliflower with some other groceries in the backseat of the car, he didn't know how he knew that either, since he didn't turn around to look in the back seat.

All of a sudden, the steering wheel in his hands turned red and gooey. All messy and drooling, it was cherry pie. A little kid's voice said, "This has to go in the garbage can, put it in the garbage." He couldn't steer cherry pie, and the gas pedal wouldn't even work right. Ahead of him on the yellow line on the road was a Pig Frog, all shining green.

And then suddenly he was standing in snow. He could see a pet shop window, and Patsy was inside. The window had a sign, "1/2 price." Patsy was standing on all four legs, but she was drooling. Whose idea was it to sell Patsy? He tried to get to the pet shop, but it was too far. In the snow there was a half stick of Juicy Fruit gum, and he bent down to pick it up, but the sun reflecting on the snow got in his eyes, and he couldn't see where the gum was, and he had to get Patsy out of the pet shop.

Then he was out of the snow and in the living room. Dr. Samuels was operating on his leg. Nick tried to tell him his leg was fine, but Dr. Samuels said, "It's going to the creek, it has worms, it's too late." Outside one of the sections of the window, a little girl was sitting on the floor with her back to him. When she turned around, he could see that it was Dianne. She looked at him and said, "What's your name?" in a little-kid voice. Nick tried to think how to tell her who he was, but she disappeared, and then his parents were in another section of the window, and his mother said, "We went to the prom, it was Beethoven." His dad waved his car keys at him and said, "Comb your hair, Ed."

Waking up, he said, Please let this be Saturday.

It was Thursday. And it was raining. And there was no dog on his bed, or even anywhere in the house.

8

His mother's note was on the kitchen table.

> To the Something Office:
>   Nick Swansen was absent from school on
> Monday, Tuesday, and Wednesday of this week. He
> wasn't something ill, but he was something some
> something something. I don't know whether or not
> you will excuse this kind of absence.
>   Something,
>   Marcia and Ralph Swansen

"I can't read some of this," he said. He was eating cereal.
"Which parts?" she asked. She had the Free Lunch mug
in her hand.
"That word." He pointed to the first unreadable word.
"Attendance."
"That one."
"Actually."

"That one."

"Experiencing."

"That one."

"I bet you can get that one, Nick." She covered up the last two letters with one finger. He looked at it. He tried to remember, and couldn't.

"It's 'personal.'"

"That one."

"Unhappiness."

"That one."

"Cordially."

Wasn't actually ill, but was experiencing some personal unhappiness. "Couldn't you say my dog bit me?"

"That didn't happen till yesterday, Nick." She folded the note and handed it to him.

He put the note in his pocket and looked out the window. Rain poured against the glass. He finished his cereal. In half an hour he'd be putting stuff in his locker. *Please* make Shana be someplace else, he said silently to somebody, maybe God.

His mother put some dishes in the sink. "How's your arm this morning, dear?" she asked. "Did you take the penicillin?"

"Yeah. It's okay." He had the pills in his pack, and he was wearing a long-sleeved shirt so everybody wouldn't ask him what was under the bandage. Maybe he could make it through the morning, and even through the afternoon, without having to go to his locker. Maybe. He took a pen from beside the telephone and put it in his pack. "Patsy's having her operation right now," he said.

"Right. And maybe she'll be home tonight. Maybe tomorrow. We'll see."

Dogs could die in surgery like anybody else. He took his pack off the chair he'd hung it on. His dad walked into the kitchen.

"Well, off to get some education, eh, Nick?" his dad said. "How about if we give you a ride? It's wet out there. Marcia, can you be ready in"—he looked at his watch—"in about ten minutes?"

"Sure," she said.

Nick wished he could go numb. He wished nothing would even touch him, even if somebody held a flaming torch against his face he wouldn't feel it. He wished he could have no color and no shape and no weight, he'd be invisible and just walk around and nobody would know he was there.

"Okay," he said.

By the time he got to Room 19, he was twelve minutes late because of standing in line at the attendance office. He stood outside the door. He would not, would *not* look at the wall where the pictures of Shana's party were. And he wouldn't look at Jill or Becky, her friends. If anybody said the word "prom," he would look in the opposite direction. He'd keep his sleeve pulled down over the bandage. He wouldn't talk unless he had to. They didn't have assigned seats, maybe he could sit next to the guy named Tom who never said anything anyway.

He held still, getting ready for the clapping. That's what they always did when somebody was out of school for a while, it was a tradition. A bunch of silly, grinning faces, getting a kick out of clapping their hands for somebody walking through a door. Patsy went through doors any time anybody opened one, and nobody clapped for her. She was getting a stainless steel pin put in her leg right this minute. He took the deepest breath he could.

He opened the door and walked in. The clapping began. He went straight to Mr. Norton, who was standing beside his desk, and handed him the attendance office paper, with UNEXCUSED stamped on it in big red letters. Somebody was saying, "There's Swansen the crook. What'd the cops get you for?" Mr. Norton took the excuse, looked at it, and put his hand on Nick's shoulder. "Welcome back, Nick," he said. "We missed you."

"You get busted yesterday? My mom saw you ridin' with cops," the voice said. It was Alex, who looked as if he didn't brush his teeth, ever. His father was the school wrestling coach, and he was always trying to talk Mr. Norton out of a hall pass to go and ask his father something. But even Alex was smart enough not to try to go to a prom.

The clapping quieted down. Mr. Norton said, "Alex, it's a contest. See if you can stop taunting Nick by the time he gets seated."

What did "taunting" mean? There was no seat beside Tom the quiet kid. Nick sat down beside Bruce, at the table that had "school = a bummer" carved in it from a long time ago. Nobody knew who carved it. Bruce elbowed him to say hello.

"Ladies and gentlemen, we're going to take up where we left off, telling what the end-of-year project is," Mr. Norton said. "Seventeen days till the deadline, you've had three days to get started, everybody should've made a final topic decision by now. Becky, you're next."

Nick didn't know if Becky was even Shana's friend anymore. Maybe Shana decided to forget everybody in Room 19. He kept his head down.

"I'm doing things you do with the preschool kids in the home ec. room," she said. Becky was gone from Room 19 some mornings, she did the preschool then.

Mr. Norton said, "Good idea, Becky. Tell us three things you do with them."

"Well . . ." Nick could hear her not knowing what to say. "Well, you teach them songs. And"—she stopped again. "Well, you do *stuff* with them. You know."

The whole room waited while she thought. When somebody was trying to think of an answer in a class discussion, Mr. Norton made everybody be quiet. Another one of his rules.

"You play games with 'em and you give 'em crayons. And you put paint smocks on 'em. And you let them stir the batter in cooking," Becky said. "Oh—and another thing. You always—you always have to—"

Another silence while Becky thought.

"You always have to tell them the painting is good, every time they make one. You know, it's just a blob or something, you always say it's a good painting. Maybe it's just a good blob." About three kids laughed.

"Sounds like a terrific idea to me," Mr. Norton said. "What about you, Jason?"

"Noah's ark. The animals and the birds. And his sons and everybody. And the dove. And Noah was six hundred years old when the flood came." Jason didn't need extra time to think, he knew what to say.

"Nobody's six hundred years old, Bartholomew. You're crazy." It was Alex talking.

"In the Bible he was," Jason said. "Hey, Mr. Norton, tell him—"

"Jason isn't crazy, Alex, and even if he were, that's not the way we talk in this room, remember? Jason, your project sounds like a good one. Bruce?"

"Yeah, what's Skateboard gonna do?" somebody said.

"I told you, the Super Bowl," Bruce said.

"That's true, you've told me, but you haven't told everybody else," said Mr. Norton. "What are you doing with the Super Bowl?"

"The scores, and who won it. And who should've won it. All the games."

"Ah, justice done at last," said Mr. Norton. "What about you, Nick?"

"Amphibians!" about eight people shouted. Nick jumped a little bit, but he still kept his head down.

Mr. Norton laughed. "Are they right, Nick?"

"Yeah," Nick said, without looking up.

"And what are you doing with them?"

"Some Oregon ones. And some others," he said. He was looking down at the table.

"And that, ladies and gentlemen, is why I like teaching this class," Mr. Norton said. "Every single person in this room has a good project to do. You're all *interested* in something. A whole roomful of good ideas, and none of them were mine. It's fun. See what I mean?"

Nick could hear some of the kids laughing and some of them muttering. He looked sideways at Bruce's football pictures.

He took another penicillin pill and then went to the library instead of eating lunch. Shana would be in the cafeteria. Along with everybody else. And somebody would say the word "prom." Patsy would be operated on by now, and she'd be sleeping it off. What do dogs dream about? Would she dream about the accident, would she feel the car hit her all over again? Would she feel the pain in the dream?

He went to the amphibians section. Just to look at pictures. In a big book he found color photographs of the Colorado River Toad. He was memorizing the warts on its hind legs when Mr. Norton sat down beside him.

"Not hungry, Nick? Or did you eat fast?"

"No," Nick said. He looked back at the Colorado River Toad.

"Listen, Nick. I'm glad you're back. I'm really glad. You were missed."

Nick didn't say anything. He kept his eyes on the book.

"You know what I think you might do with your project this year?"

"What?"

"I think you could make it a book. To teach kids about amphibians. If you don't use the fancy words, just put it all in your own words, and do your own drawings—can you do it without the big words?"

"I don't know."

"Well, try." He looked at the open book on the table. "There's one," he pointed. "'Paratoid.' What in the world does that mean?"

"Don't you know?" Nick looked sideways, a little, not very much.

Mr. Norton laughed. "Of course I don't. You and Mr.

Wakamatsu are probably the only ones on this campus who do. What is it?"

"It's a thing at the back of a toad's head, it looks kind of like a wart but it's a gland."

"That's what I mean. Your own words are fine. If you draw this toad, and you label that thing just the way you said it, 'looks kind of like a wart but it's a gland,' kids would understand. Maybe even I would. You've got seventeen days. Think you can do that?"

"I don't know." He turned the page, to the Sonoran Green Toad, which has a yellowish green and black pattern.

"Well, I'm suggesting you try. That way, you'll be writing your own amphibian book. Think about it, okay? Make a mind note?"

"Okay."

Mr. Norton didn't leave. "That's not what I came over here to say, Nick. I came over here to tell you I know that walking in that door this morning was one of the hardest things you may ever have done."

Nick looked down at the place where the two pages came together in the book. He wanted to be air. No weight, no anything.

"Can you look at me, Nick?"

Nick had looked at cops and a veterinarian and Patsy's broken leg and at a gearshift he didn't know how to use, he'd looked at a cross-eyed doctor bandaging his arm and at his parents when they thought about him being killed and then they'd have nobody left at all; he'd looked at his watch at the prom and wondered when Shana was coming, while people danced and kissed in their formal clothes. He'd looked at the Hindu cummerbund and the rest of the ridiculous tuxedo falling on the floor where he'd thrown it, he'd looked at his own vomit as he tried to clean it up. He'd looked into a smear of sun reflected in a mirror held by somebody who wanted him to wreck his mother's car. He'd looked at Dianne dead again in his nightmare.

He looked at Mr. Norton.

At his brown eyes and streak of brown hair that was always falling over his forehead, and at his mouth that broke into laughing when everybody was being too serious, like the thing about mothers with their hands on everybody's foreheads looking for fever. He wasn't laughing now.

"I know walking in that door this morning took a whole lot of guts. That's all I wanted to say."

He got up and walked away.

Mr. Norton knew about the prom, then. He must know. Nick didn't know if he felt better or worse about everything when Mr. Norton walked away. All he knew was that he wanted to be invisible.

In Room 19, Nick's sleeve slid up while Mr. Norton was giving the after-lunch quiz. (If you were in Room 19 a year ago, name one end-of-year project you remember besides your own—no fair writing "Skateboard," everybody remembers that. Think of one thing you know now that you didn't know last week. Would you rather visit Ireland or China, and why?)

Bruce whispered, "Hey, Swansen, what happened to your arm?"

Nick didn't want to say anything. He whispered back, "Guess."

"Alligator jumped off a sweater and bit you."

114

Nick thought of a little tiny alligator jumping like a grasshopper off somebody's sweater and taking little bites in his arm. Little tiny teeth, and little tiny growling sounds. He imagined Dr. Willis with her crossed eye, bandaging alligator bites. And the mustached policeman saying, "Alligator bite you, Ed?"

And he laughed. He couldn't remember the last time he'd laughed at anything. Did he laugh when he was drinking the whiskey? He couldn't remember.

"You gotta build a pen for 'em," Bruce whispered. "Put 'em on a leash if you take 'em for walks. Didn't anybody ever tell you that?"

"Windows, you two. Bruce and Nick. Three each. After you turn in your quizzes," Mr. Norton said. He hardly ever got upset, he just assigned cleanup jobs. "No more than seven minutes." If he didn't put a time limit on the cleanup job, somebody could pretend to take all afternoon to do it.

While they squirted and wiped the windows, Nick whispered to Bruce part of what happened. He left out the part about the cop calling him Ed. Bruce kept laughing, trying not to make any noise. "Man, that's funny," he whispered.

"It's not your dog," Nick whispered back.

"You really drove your mom's car?"

"Sort of."

"Man." Bruce shook his head. "That's rugged." They finished the windows, and Bruce made a face at the fish in the aquarium as he walked past it. Then he stopped at Becky's chair, pointed with his thumb over his shoulder at the windows, and said, "Pretty good blobs, huh?"

Becky told him to go away and went on writing.

They put away the window cleaning stuff and sat

down. Nick slumped in his chair. He was back in Room 19, that was for sure.

"How come you stayed home all that time?" Bruce whispered.

"None of your business," Nick whispered back.

"Stop being a jerk, Swansen."

"Stop bothering me."

"Jerk."

Nick didn't say anything.

"Kerby trashed you, didn't she?" Bruce whispered.

Nick looked down at the table. He felt jagged. He said to himself, people are round, they've got round organs and round eyeballs and almost everything in them is round, and I'm jagged, I've got jagged edges. Like a sawblade. He looked at the carved "s" in "school = a bummer." It had pink eraser shreds in it. For years, people had sat at this table and tried to erase things they didn't want anybody to see.

He whispered to Bruce, "Can I borrow your math book?" He was surprised he'd got the words out.

"Sure." Even whispering, Bruce said it in a way that kind of sounded as if he was forgiving somebody for something. He reached into a pile of books on the table and handed the math book to Nick.

When school was out, Nick gave everybody ten minutes to clear out of the halls before he went to his locker. He couldn't stay away from it for the rest of his life, it had his math book and other stuff he needed.

School was out at 3:03, for no reason he understood. School never did anything on the hour or half hour. What was Patsy doing now? At 3:13, he went to his locker. Only a few kids were hanging around. Somebody came by and said, "Hey, what you got in that pack, training wheels?"

"Amphibian books," Nick said. The boy walked on down the hall.

Once in a while people tried to get Special Ed. kids that way. Sometimes Room 19 had class discussions about it, if somebody came in crying or mad. Most of the kids voted with Mr. Norton that the best thing to do was just give a straight answer. You could do other things, like punch them out or ignore them. If you punched somebody out, you got kicked out of school for three days. And ignoring them was too hard sometimes, depending on what they said. Once a kid faked knocking Jason Bartholomew on the head, like knocking on a door, and said, "Nobody home." Jason punched him out. Mr. Norton talked to the principal about it, but Jason still got three days.

Nick opened his locker. Piles of books, papers, and gym clothes fell out on the floor. The gym clothes were from last Friday. He'd forgotten to take them home to be washed. They smelled from being stuffed in the locker for so long. Last Friday he had his mind on the prom. An unfinished math assignment fell out. And a book on toads that Mr. Wakamatsu had let him borrow.

He had to sort out the junk and he had to call Dr. Samuels about Patsy. He could use his lunch money for the pay phone.

But he couldn't remember Dr. Samuels's number. He should have copied it down this morning and put it in his pocket. Jerk. He didn't know how to spell it, so he couldn't look it up. Maybe his parents had already called about Patsy anyway. He tried to call his dad's office. He got a busy signal.

He tried Free Lunch. He got a busy signal. He tried them both again. Same thing.

He walked outside.

The air was cleaned up after the rain. As he looked around, it was almost as if a lens was standing up straight in front of him. He could see the sharp outlines of things, like the place where the corner of the building ended and the sky began. And like where a squirrel was standing a few feet away, staring at the bark of a tree on the lawn: Nick could see its eyes. And instead of heading for home, he walked toward the gym. He didn't know why he was going to go running. All he knew was that he was going to do it. Maybe it was because Bruce just lent him his math book and didn't ask him anything more. Maybe it was because Shana knew she was a stinkpot and stayed away from her locker after school. Maybe he was going running for no reason.

In the locker room, he put on his shorts and jersey. The jersey sleeves were cut off short, but he wasn't going to see anybody he'd have to explain the bandage to. From the gym to the track was about as far as half of a city block, and it was grass. While you walked across it, you could think about how far or how fast you were going to run. Today it had some violets growing. Nobody planted them, they just grew. If you tried not to step on them you'd have to walk crooked, they were all over the place. He didn't know how many laps he was going to do. Maybe a mile. Maybe more, maybe less. Four laps were about a mile.

Some puddles were left from the rain. Nick went to the outside lane and felt his legs go into motion. He felt as if he'd been sitting in one place for days. Two other people were sprinting. Nick didn't sprint. He was an endurance runner. The gym teacher had told him once, "Nick, you've got endurance."

When you ran on the track, you could see Mt. Hood with its snow shining. Even when you had your back to the mountain, you knew you'd round a curve pretty soon and there it would be, staring you in the face. Also, there were some evergreen trees near the track, in bunches, and you could hear some birds.

Dr. Willis had stood on top of Mt. Hood and looked down cross-eyed at the world. Instead of being an astronaut. People died sometimes climbing it. You could fall into a crevasse and die before anybody knew where you were. Nick went skiing there, but you couldn't see where he skied, it was below the glaciers. Last time he went, he only fell down three times.

He was on the third lap, on the curve, at the far end of the gym, where you could see the mountain standing up high. The two sprinters stopped and went toward the gym. He was alone on the track, as if it was his track. A girl was sitting on the top row of the bleachers with a book, maybe she was doing homework. Nobody else was around. He saw his shadow being pushed ahead of him, and he tried to see whether the shadow looked jagged, or sort of rounded like everybody else's. He couldn't tell; it was just a shadow sliding along the track. The girl on the bleachers waved to him, and he waved back. She had short hair like a boy's.

He kept running. What was Patsy doing right now? He rounded another curve. Fourth lap. Maybe he would run more than a mile. As he passed the part of the bleachers where the girl was sitting, she pointed to her arm and then to him. He didn't know what she meant. Like asking somebody what time it was. He could tell her when he stopped running, if she still wanted to know. You could never tell what girls were thinking, anyway.

He kept running. He listened to the sound of his shoes hitting the track, and to his breathing, and he watched his shadow appear and disappear as he rounded the curves. He didn't think about anything, he just ran.

After seven laps, or maybe it was eight, he decided to stop. He'd take a long shower, and he wouldn't think there, either. It felt good not to think.

As he slowed to a walk, he saw the girl walk down the bleachers with her book under her arm. She was wearing a shirt with big maroon and white stripes going across it, he could see the stripes even from a distance. She took long steps, and her wide blue skirt kind of bounced in the air with each step. Quitting time for everybody. He breathed hard and felt the muscles in his legs tingle from running. He wiped his face with the edge of his jersey and headed for the gym.

"Hi, Nick."

He turned around. The sun was in his eyes. He put his hand up to shield them and squinted at her. And then he turned away and started toward the gym again. Maybe he was wrong, maybe it was somebody else. Her hair was all cut off short.

"I thought you were never coming back. What happened to your arm?" she said.

He stopped walking but he kept his back to her. He felt his legs start to shake. He could go right ahead to the gym and get into the shower and pretend she wasn't there. He had to find out about Patsy. He had homework to do. He'd spent five weird days because of her, and there she was, standing on the grass, holding a book in her hand and asking him a question. What would be the right thing to do? He said to himself, I've spent my whole life trying to do the right thing, and I'm sick of it.

He turned partway around and saw her shape against the sun. "Go jump off a cliff," he said. Then he went on walking across the grass. He knew it was a rotten thing to say to somebody. He said it anyway.

"Listen, Nick, I have to tell you what happened—" She was walking beside him. "You have to listen to me."

He kept walking, staring straight ahead. He could feel her stop, stand still on the grass, and then run to catch up with him.

"See, I saw the box of flowers in the refrigerator, and I—what happened to your arm?"

He said to himself, Swansen, are you gonna keep on walking, or are you gonna stop? He kept walking.

"Nick, I have to talk to you. I have to tell you—Nicholas, will you stop?" She ran a little bit to catch up. She was sort of jogging beside him, in skinny white sandals. Out of the corner of his right eye he could see her blue skirt bouncing in front of her. "Will you please *listen* to me?"

He stopped walking and backed away about four feet. He looked at her forehead. He remembered watching her long, bendy hair burn over his wastebasket, sizzling and making little tiny flares, and then disappear.

"Nick, I've figured out where Up is."

He looked at her eyes for just a second, and then looked past her at the bleachers.

"It's where you flunk tests all the time, and everybody wants you to be so smart all the time, it's so much faster—listen, do you ever flunk tests in Room 19?"

He'd never flunked one, but he didn't have to tell her that. It was none of her business. "What happened to your hair?" he said.

She put her hand up to the side of her head. "It's ugly, isn't it?"

Nick didn't know if it was ugly, it was just short and crooked.

"Is it really ugly, Nick?" She sounded as if she didn't know the answer.

"I don't know."

"I wanted to call you, I kept going to the phone, and every time, I just put it down in the middle of punching the buttons, I couldn't—you know?"

No, he didn't know. When did she try to call and she couldn't? Sunday? Tuesday? Maybe while he was throwing up?

"No." He wiped his face again with the front of his jersey. When he took it down from his face, he could see her looking at his bandaged arm. He moved it so it was sort of behind him.

"Nick, you don't know how hard this is—come on, I'm trying—" She drooped her shoulders, the way you do when you're thinking about giving up.

He looked down at the front of his jersey, all blotched and wet from wiping his face.

"The pink roses are beautiful, listen, I wasn't gonna tell you this . . ."

He just looked at her. He saw himself wheeling his bike

out of the flower shop, backwards, with the corsage in its box in the basket.

"I wear the corsage all the time at home, don't tell anybody." She sat cross-legged on the grass and pulled her skirt down over her knees.

Shana walked around her house, part of it gloomy like a haunted house and part of it in magazine pictures, and she was wearing a wrist corsage of pink unfolded rosebuds, holding her arm up out of the way of everything. Did she roller-skate around the kitchen wearing the flowers on her wrist? Maybe he was supposed to get mad that she did that, went around the house wearing the flowers he bought with the greenhouse money.

"Aren't you gonna say anything?" she asked.

He looked down at her.

She stuck her hands out like flippers, one hand with the book in it. She put her hands down on the grass. "Sit down. Will you sit down, Nick?"

He looked at the grass. It was still damp from the rain. The afternoon sun was shining on the violets. He should just walk away. He had things to do. He looked at Shana's chopped-off hair. He sat down. "What happened to your hair?" he asked.

"That's what I'm trying to explain. See, I saw the flowers in the refrigerator, and I—I went to the hairdresser, I was having my hair done for the prom—"

"Why'd you have it all cut off?"

"I didn't. She didn't cut any of it off. She put it on top of my head, it had curls hanging down partway, long ones, it looked—and I had a ribbon to go with the color of my dress and she put it in my hair, it was—I didn't cut it off till way later."

Nick looked at his socks. He pulled his left leg up and tied his shoe. It didn't need tying. He didn't think he should listen to her.

"So, I went home, and I saw the flowers in the refrigerator, and Nancy was helping me finish the dress, and everything was a mess, and Nancy and my mother got so—see, I made this mistake, and the dress turned out bad—this is terrible. . . ." Her voice faded out.

"Nancy who?" He didn't even care, it was just something to say. He looked across the grass at a fat robin working a worm out of the ground.

"Nancy in algebra, you don't know her, I guess. She saw this terrible mess—see, I sewed the whole skirt of the dress wrong, then my mother got all excited and Nancy started ripping out the seam, well, all four seams, you can't even see anything at the sewing machine, it's all dark but just one lamp—my mother had to go to this party and she grabbed the dress from Nancy and she put it on the machine, and I was trying to hold the material up off the floor, there's junk all over the floor, my parents are remodeling—"

She stopped, like being tired, or not knowing how to tell it. Nick didn't know how you make a dress, but he could see Shana and her mother and some other girl jumping around the sewing machine in that dark room. He looked at his shoes.

"And my mother had these people taking pictures of the kitchen, and they wouldn't leave, it was getting late, my mother left the sewing machine with the dress hanging on it, and—" Shana was trying to show him with her hands everything going wrong. "Nancy, see, Nancy tried, she sat down and started on the other side of the skirt, she said she could fix it—then everything happened wrong. My mother came back and she had this red wine in a glass, and she put it on the end of the sewing machine, and of course it spilled on the dress when the cat put his claws on the material hanging down from the dress—I mean the half-dress, it wasn't even a dress . . ."

Nick was trying to follow the story, it was like a movie where the film keeps slipping on the projector.

"See, I flunked the algebra test the day before, and Mom and Dad didn't get mad or anything right away. So, when Nancy grabbed the part of the dress with the wine on it—she said we had to put it in the washer and sew it together later—then she had to go home to get dressed for the prom, and my mother started yelling we couldn't wash it yet, it wasn't finished—it was like the Three Stooges, I'm not kidding."

Shana pulled up a clump of grass and held it in her fist. Then she started pulling blades of grass out of the fist with her other hand and laying them on her skirt, one at a time. Nick watched her hands.

"So. By the time it was out of the washer my mother was taking a shower, she had to go to some party, her hair was wet, we had to put it in the dryer, I mean the half-dress—and then my dad came in and he said it was my stupid fault for the stupid mistake I made when I sewed the skirt, he said I should study harder for the algebra test instead, and I said I couldn't do everything at once, so we had a fight and I."

Shana stopped talking. She kept pulling blades of grass out of her fist one by one and putting them on her skirt. She had them lined up like a green fence all across her lap.

"I promised I wouldn't cry, telling you. And I'm not." She added three more blades of grass to the fence. "Am I?" She put her fist full of grass on her knee.

He had to look at her face to tell her whether she was or not. "No," he said. Then he looked back down at the wet grass.

"I don't know, first I'm in Room 19, then I'm not in Room 19. I don't know if I'll flunk the next algebra test too. My parents had a fight 'cause my dad said I was stupid—that was later, like the next day or something—So: I told my mother to just forget it, you called while she was in the shower, we weren't going to the prom."

Nick looked at Shana's face again. You could just go around, wearing your same face day after day, and all the time you could be lying to people, and nobody might know. You could just keep on doing it all your life. A whole human race of liars.

"I wish you'd say something, Nick. Just something."

He kept looking at her. He was thinking about how many people there must be in the world, all lying their heads off. Except babies. You couldn't count babies.

She shrugged her shoulders. "I didn't cut my hair off till the next day. I just got mad at everything and I cut it all off. I know it's disgusting."

He looked at her chopped hair. He thought about Mr. Kerby telling her she was stupid about sewing and algebra, and the cat spilling red wine on the dress, and pictures of their kitchen in a magazine, all bright-colored. And Shana making up the lie and then cutting her hair off crooked the next day. "No," he said.

"But I didn't cut it at first. First I made two lists.

Norton's lists. Things that went wrong and things that went right. The wrong list went a whole page. *Then* I cut it." She put more blades of grass in the fence on her skirt. "I mean my hair. Cut my hair," she said. And she suddenly swept her right hand across her skirt and blew away the whole grass fence.

"And my parents are fighting, it's mostly 'cause of what I did. I'm grounded, I'm not even supposed to be here now, I'm supposed to go right home after school. It's my minimal brain dysfunction that's got me into all this mess. I never want to see a lavender dress again in my life. Did you ever wish you could just disappear? You know, be invisible or something?"

Nick looked at her. Yes. He did. This morning, and all day today, except the part about the alligator bites. And it was because of her. And now she was sitting right here on the grass, asking him if he'd ever wanted to. He felt weird and jumbled. "Your what?" he asked.

"What do you mean, my what?"

"What you said about your brain."

"My minimal brain dysfunction."

"What's that?"

She looked at him. "Don't you know? Where've you been? Minimal *brain* dysfunction. It's what puts people in Room 19. Some people, I mean. You've probably got it, too. I mean, you haven't got Downs, you're not retarded or anything—you probably have it."

"What does it mean?" "Probably" was a word he wanted to throw into the Columbia River and have it disappear.

"I don't know. My brain just isn't regular. You know. I flunk tests and stuff. I've got a reading problem. And I can't

127

remember stuff like everybody else. What happened to your arm?"

"Minimal brain what?" he asked.

"Dysfunction. Means something's not connecting upstairs. You know."

"Dysfunction," he said. There was a name for it. Nick said to himself, Why should I tell her what happened to my arm? Somewhere in that big old house she could've found a dress to wear. She didn't have to make up a lie and make me wait for hours and hours like a drooler while everybody danced to the music.

She really just didn't want to go to the prom with somebody in Room 19. He said to himself, I've got minimal brain something.

"It's a long story," he said.

"Is that why you stayed out of school for three days?"

He looked at her. He could make up a lie and say Patsy bit him on Sunday. Why not? He looked down at the grass. He picked a violet that was growing near his knee. The stem was about two inches long. If you had a microscope you could look down inside the violet and see all its parts, clear down to where they started, the place where they were just one part all together, before they separated. Why not tell Shana a lie? He looked down into the flower.

"No. That's not why. My dog didn't bite me till yesterday. It wasn't her fault. She got hit by a car. It's a long story."

The sun was going down behind the bleachers.

Shana looked at him as if she was trying to figure something out. Then she said, "Your own dog bit you? You have stitches?"

"No. I mean yes, but no stitches." He held the violet

stem between his thumb and finger and spun it back and forth so it twirled. "I've gotta go home and call the vet. She had a pin put in her leg, I've gotta find out if she can come home." He got up off the ground. His shorts were wet from the grass. He dropped the violet on the ground.

"I've gotta go home and get yelled at," Shana said. She picked up the violet and her book and stood up.

Nick started toward the gym.

"Hey, Nick," she said.

He turned around.

"You gonna run tomorrow?"

"I don't know."

"Well, do you *think* you are?"

"Maybe. Why?"

"Because I want to run with you. Can I?"

He watched her brush the damp grass off the back of her skirt. People were always asking him questions. Shana asked too many questions. She didn't want to dance with him, but she wanted to run with him. He felt two words, Yes and No, in the back part of his mind, with a kind of jagged wall between them. If he said one of them, he should be saying the other one. Either one would be a wrong answer.

"I don't know," he said.

She crossed her arms in front of her stomach, holding the book in one hand and the violet in the other. Both her hands were in fists. "Well, if you do run, will you do it right after school?"

"Yeah."

She looked back at the bleachers, then she looked at him. She turned the book sideways against her stomach.

"I'll meet you on the track. I'll see if I can trade something for being grounded. Garbage and mowing the lawn or something."

He turned toward the gym. He saw the letters O.K. in his mind. He wondered if you could invent an answer that didn't say either yes or no.

"Hey, Nick," she called.

He turned around again.

"You stayed out of school for something else. Not the dog. Right?"

She was putting her hand up like running it through her hair, but there was hardly any to run it through. She was still holding the violet in that hand. He couldn't make his voice say anything. He turned around and went to the gym. He had to take a shower and make sure he didn't get his left arm wet and then get home fast. He should have been home a long time ago to see about Patsy.

Bruce said, "Kerby trashed you, didn't she?" Nick heard him say it again in his mind. And then he thought about Shana's father calling her stupid. That was why he didn't know what answer to say when she asked him about running tomorrow.

At the door to the locker room he looked back. Shana was standing on the grass. She hadn't moved. She was looking at him.

9

When Nick walked in the door, Patsy was standing in the hallway looking at him. Her splint was huge. More like a cast. How could she walk in such a thing? Could she walk at all? Seeing her almost amazed him.

"Hey, Pats, you're home." He put his pack on the floor and put his arms around her neck. She wobbled a little. "How's it feel?"

"Nick, where've you been? Why are you so late?" His mother came into the hallway. "She looks pretty good, doesn't she? For having surgery."

"Yeah," he said. "Hey, Pats, can you walk?" He backed away. "Come on, Pats, come here." She limped toward him. "Good girl. That's great."

"She can't get up the stairs, though. Inside and out, yes. She can manage a couple of steps. All the way upstairs, no."

"I'll sleep downstairs with her."

"Where've you been, Nick?"

"I went running."

"Really? Good for you. Shall I ask how school was?"

"It was okay. Here, can you wash my gym stuff for tomorrow?" He reached into his pack to get it out.

"You know perfectly well how to do laundry, Nick. I'll give you some other white things to put with it."

While he listened to the laundry go *smoosh*—smoosh—*smoosh*—smoosh, Nick said things over to himself: dress ruined, lie told, minimal something, brain something, Patsy home, run tomorrow, chopped hair, penicillin, brain something, minimal something, drooler jerk—and he realized he was saying the things in time to the washer. What a drooler thing to do.

That night, he worked on amphibians. He spread the things on the living room floor so he could be with Patsy. If he looked up at the window, he could see them together in one frame of it. He started with the Pig Frog because people would like its color. While he was working on it, his dad came in and sat down on the floor, facing him. You could tell by the way he sat down that he had a speech to make.

"Nick, I want to tell you I know it was hard to go to school today. Your mother and I understand how hard it was."

They didn't. Nick kept on listening.

"And I'm not angry about the clutch in Mom's car. It wasn't exactly the right thing to do, but it was *a* thing to do. It was an idea—not a perfect idea, but an idea. How does your arm feel tonight? You taking the pills?"

"It's okay. Yeah."

"Driving lesson Saturday, right?"

"Yeah."

His father looked at the amphibian things on the floor.

He stroked Patsy, who was lying beside the Pig Frog with her splint covering all of the salamanders. He got up, walked around the room, played a sort of little tune on the piano, and came back and sat down again. "Nick. Uh—did you, uh—" He brushed some dog hairs off the Sonoran Green Toad. "Did you see Shana today?"

"Yeah," Nick said. He didn't look up.

"Did you talk to her?"

"Yeah."

"You don't want to tell me what she said, do you?"

Nick looked at his dad. He thought about watching him floating alder cones on thimbleberry leaves down the creek, and then about being carried up the bank through the stickers, and about the Juicy Fruit gum. "No," he said.

"That's okay, Nick." He ran his hand over the amphibian chart again. "I just want you to know your mom and I think you've got courage. That's all."

Nick looked at his dad. Then he went back to the Pig Frog.

It was a warm night. Nick decided to sleep in the back-yard with Patsy because she couldn't go upstairs. He got the air mattress out of his closet and blew it up, then he asked his mother where another one was, for Patsy to sleep on. She couldn't fit on one with him, especially with her big splint. They had four air mattresses, from when they used to go camping, when Dianne was alive.

His mother said it was in the basement, and she said she was glad he and Patsy were going to sleep outside. "Both of you with bandages, both of you sleeping under the stars—that's nice, Nick. It's really nice."

Mothers. You could keep them sort of happy if every-thing was always nice. And there were those things you weren't supposed to do: don't get hurt, don't get dirty, don't get drunk, don't get scared. If you did any of those, things wouldn't be nice and your mother would get all upset.

Lying in the backyard, Nick could see the forsythia branches with their bright yellow blooms hanging in curves, like water from a fountain, at the edge of the yard, near the fence. The light from his parents' bedroom window was shining on the grass, making a path to the bushes. He heard his parents talking, their window was open. He heard the words dog, Free Lunch, school, dentist, taxes, Special Ed. He couldn't make out anything else. He thought of yelling up at their window, "I've got minimal brain something, that's why—" But he couldn't remember the word. Their light went out. The forsythia blossoms turned white against the black.

When he still went to school with Roger and Anthony, they slept in Roger's backyard one night. They mixed up a chocolate cake mix and ate it out of the bowl with three big spoons, and it made them feel sick, and they laughed. They got the batter on their sleeping bags, and Roger's mother got upset. It was fun. Then he went to fourth grade in Special Ed. And Roger and Anthony disappeared. They were both sixteen now, too. Maybe they played on a foot-ball team somewhere. Two different teams, they went to two different places. He wondered: Do Roger and Anthony walk down the halls of their schools now, asking Special Ed. kids if they have training wheels in their packs, or knocking them on the head and saying, "Nobody home"?

He lay on his back in the sleeping bag, listening to the branches of the dogwood tree waving, and looked up at the stars. They looked like petals of white clover that somebody had thrown into the sky. But they were in designs. Each of the designs was a little part of the whole big thing, and how far did the whole thing go? If you looked at the part of the sky you could see, you could times it by two, that would be double. Then you could times it by two again, and it would be double what you had before. You could keep on doing it till you could imagine the size of the universe, but your brain would give up before you got the answer.

He turned over on his stomach. The sound he made was like somebody just turning over in a sleeping bag on an air mattress. Sort of regular. He realized he didn't feel quite as jagged as before. Not completely even all over, the way you should be, but not quite as jagged, either. There was a name for what he was, minimal brain something. Was it better or worse to have a name for what you were? He didn't know.

He pulled his right arm out of the sleeping bag and put his hand on Patsy's neck. He could feel her breathing.

Friday, the last day of school for the week. Nick looked around Room 19 and tried to decide who had the minimal brain thing. It was hard to know. Jason Bartholomew, maybe. The quiet kid named Tom, you couldn't tell because he never said anything. Becky and Jill, maybe. Not the two Down's kids, they had Down's. Dick and Beverly. You could tell they had Down's when you looked at them. In one way they were lucky, because if somebody tried to get them, like the kid who asked about the training wheels, or like the kid who knocked Jason Bartholomew on the head, Dick and Beverly usually didn't know what was going on. They usually just smiled. Alex, who said that thing about the cops yesterday, he must have the minimal brain thing. But maybe more of it. And he was kind of like the hyperactives they had in sixth grade. Did Shana's minimal brain thing get better so she went Up? She studied very hard in Room 19 all the time when she was there, she didn't sit around and cut paper designs. He looked at Bruce. Did Bruce have it?

Nick worked on the Oregon Slender Sal part of his project. Maybe he would make it into a book. Maybe that was a good idea.

Jason Bartholomew came to lean over Nick's shoulder and watch. "You still think God didn't make that lizard?" he asked.

"It's a salamander," Nick said.

"You still think people came from fish?" Jason said.

Nick looked up at him. Explaining it to Jason would be impossible. "Why don't you go back to your flood?" Nick said.

"Hey, Jason, I've got two giraffes, you want 'em for your ark?" Jill was holding up a magazine. Jason walked away to see if he wanted the giraffes.

Nick looked at Mr. Norton, who was helping Alex make a list of something. Mr. Norton looked up. He smiled at Nick and just barely nodded his head. Then he did the same thing at Jason and Jill, and went back to helping Alex. Mr. Norton knew who had the minimal brain thing and who didn't, but you couldn't tell by looking at his face. Nick went back to the Oregon Slender Sal.

After school, he changed into his running stuff and went to the outside lane. The track was empty. Maybe Shana wouldn't show up. She didn't show up at the prom, why should she show up on the track? Except she said she would. But she said she'd go to the prom, too. And the running was her idea. But she could change her mind. Maybe her new friends would laugh at her for going running with a drooler. Maybe she decided to trash him again.

But she said she'd be there.

Don't count on it, Swansen, he said to himself, and he started to run toward Mt. Hood. He could add something to the list of things you weren't supposed to do. Don't get hurt, don't get dirty, don't get drunk, don't get scared, don't count on it. You ended up doing all of them.

He ran two laps. Mt. Hood had a cloud like a baseball cap on top of it. When you turned your back to the mountain, the cloud moved a little, and when you came around the curve again you could see it in a different place.

There she was. Running toward the track and waving both her arms. She had running stuff on. She didn't lie. She didn't change her mind. Nick slowed down.

"My parents are gonna have a fit again," she said, and went to the middle lane. "But I passed the English test, that's why I'm late, I had to see what I got. I got a C. Pretty hot stuff, for me. How's your dog?" She got in stride with him.

He looked out of the corner of his left eye at her. He decided not to run as fast as yesterday. She did look strange with her hair chopped. She had strong legs, they looked nice when she ran.

"She's okay. She's got a big splint, she can't go upstairs," he said.

"How's Room 19?"

"It's okay."

"This is the first time I don't have to do the end-of-year project," she said. They ran along for a while, past the bleachers. "I have to take tests all the time instead."

Nick didn't say anything.

"It's weird," she said.

"What is?"

"Oh, everything. Well, not everything. Most things." They ran along and she didn't talk. Then she did. "I guess all the kids in my classes know I came from Room 19. They know I went Up to get there, they were already there."

They ran without talking again.

"And if I flunk a test I have to hide my paper fast so nobody sees it. You know. People all stand around and they talk about what they got, and you have to pretend you have to go someplace right away, or you forgot to get a book at the library. It makes you feel like a criminal or something."

It was Nick's fourth lap, Shana's second. The baseball cap on top of the mountain had flattened out and lay floating flat just above the peak.

"But it's okay, being Up, isn't it?" Nick said. "I mean better than Room 19?" He meant she didn't have to look at droolers all day.

She didn't say anything for a few strides. "I don't know. Yeah. It's okay. Sometimes it's great." They ran some more. "And then it's not okay. Sometimes it's not okay at all."

She sounded like Dr. Willis. That part about not okay.

"Shana?"

"Yeah?"

"You still have the minimal brain thing, right? It didn't go away?"

"Dysfunction. Yeah, I still have it. It doesn't go away. You always have it."

They ran some more. They both sounded a little bit out of breath when they talked. "It's like being born with one arm or something. It doesn't go away," she said. "You can work hard to try to make up for it, but it's there."

Nick turned to look at her. She was still pretty, even without the long hair. She had curls put in her hair for the prom. They hung down partway from the top of her head when she had her hair put up there. He tried to see in his mind what they looked like. He couldn't. Running along, she had her mouth open the way you do when you run, and you could hear the little puffs of breath coming out like steam from a little tiny train. She wasn't really smiling, but her face was sort of even-looking. He didn't know the words for it.

"But then, you're a savant, too. So that helps a little bit," Shana said, puffing little puffs of air.

"I'm a what?"

"A savant. Your old frogs and things. You know all about them, you can name them in your sleep. Remember that guy from two years ago, he knew everything about the Rolling Stones, he knew every song and when they were recorded? He even knew all the words. He was one, too."

Nick remembered him. He wore the same thing every day, a green plaid shirt and jeans. But he wasn't dirty. Maybe he had a hundred green plaid shirts. Nick started laughing.

"What's so funny?"

"His shirt."

"Right!" Shana laughed. "Green plaid. Poor guy. I don't think he even knew he always wore the same thing."

"I wonder what his name was," Nick said.

"I don't know. I've lost it."

"Me too."

They ran along. Nick thought about Shana's green balloon in March at the Going Up party, it was kind of like the green of some of the bushes at the side of the track with the sun shining on them. It was the kind of thought he wouldn't even let himself think yesterday, or all week, even. Like a poison thought or something. Now it wasn't so terrible, he just went ahead and thought it.

"Hey, Shana," he said.

"What?"

"What was that kid's name, the shoplifter? The one that morked hard?"

"I don't know. Jack, maybe. Maybe Jake."

"Maybe Jim?" Nick was hunting in his mind.

"John?" Shana said.

They were both puffing and saying names of somebody who'd disappeared and they'd never see him again and it was suddenly funny. Bruce would think it was a big joke.

"Jeff?" Nick said, laughing.

"Jasper?" Shana laughed, too.

Nick looked at their shadows, sliding along with their heads and arms shaking at a joke. "I don't think so," he said. "Maybe Josh?"

"Nope. He didn't look like a Josh."

They went on running. Nick asked, "Shana, what's that word? The one where you know about one thing? Like that Rolling Stones guy?"

"You mean savant?"

"Yeah. Say it again."

"Sa—vahnt. How do you know so much about amphibians, Nick?"

"I don't know. How do you know all about the savant and the minimal brain thing?"

"Norton told me."

"He never told me."

"He won't tell you if you don't ask him. I asked him. And Becky and Jill."

"When?"

"I don't know. When he wouldn't let the Rolling Stones kid sing the songs in school. We just decided to ask him why that guy knew so much about one thing if he was Special Ed. And he told us. It's kind of not fair, he tells your parents but he won't tell you till you ask."

They were quiet for a while. How many laps? Nick had lost track. He wasn't even very tired. He ran faster yesterday.

"Becky and Jill and I tried to figure out why you get minimal brain dysfunction or why you have Down's. We tried to figure out which kids have to be Special Ed.—the older or the younger. Or the middle. Becky has two regular brothers, they're older. And Jill's sister, she's a freshman, she isn't Special Ed. And Bruce has a little brother. Jason has three sisters, all younger. Alex has two sisters, one older and one younger. And the Down's kids, one of 'em has a brother and one of 'em is an only child. And then there's me. I don't have any brothers or sisters. And there's you, you don't either. So you can't tell who's gonna be Special Ed. Sometimes it's somebody with other kids in the family, sometimes it's an only child like you. Or me."

Nick looked at Shana. The sun was getting lower in the sky, and it made her legs look kind of golden. Not really like gold, but sort of golden.

"I used to have a sister," he said. He wasn't sure why he said it, it just came out. Telling her might be a terrible thing to do; he might get the dream again. But he never had it twice in one week. He hardly ever told people about his sister. Bruce knew. Not many others. Roger and Anthony knew, of course. They knew the next day.

"What do you mean, you used to have one? She decide not to be your sister anymore or something?"

"She died."

"Oh," Shana said. She slowed down. Nick couldn't even see her shadow.

She caught up with him again. "That's a tragedy, Nick," she said.

"I know it. She was little, she was ten."

Nick told her about the swimming pool. It took just a little bit more than one lap to tell her. He couldn't have explained why he told her, he just did. It was maybe his ninth lap, maybe his tenth. He also told her about Dianne reading *James and the Giant Peach* to him, and about the game they used to play where Dianne was Rabbit and he was Winnie-the-Pooh. And sometimes Dianne was Christopher Robin and he had to be Roo, Kanga's baby. He left out the part about hitting Dianne to try to make her breathe when she was already drowned. You'd never tell anybody about that.

Shana listened to the whole thing without talking. Then she said, "So you moved out of that house and everything?"

142

"Yeah."

"Is that why you moved out of that house?"

"I don't know." Maybe there were other reasons.

"Your parents must feel terrible."

"I think so."

"Do you think about her a lot?"

Nobody ever asked him that. "Yeah. No. I do, but not all the time. I have a—never mind." He wouldn't tell her about the dream, of course.

They ran one whole lap without talking. Then Shana said, "Do you think we've done two miles? I'm getting tired."

"Yeah. I think so."

"I should stop. I've got piles of homework. It's Friday, but my mom and dad are still gonna do their yelling." They slowed down. "I tried explaining yesterday, but they still yelled. They take turns. I'm still grounded. But now I've got the laundry and the lawn mowing *and* the vacuuming."

Nick looked at her. It was all because of what she did about the prom. "Are they mad that you cut your hair?" he asked.

"Yeah. That, too. Mom said it's the ugliest thing she ever saw."

They slowed to a walk. She said, "If you want to know what I think, I think the new kitchen is kind of ugly, too."

"Your kitchen's nice," he said.

"It's nice if you like never being able to spill anything. You ever hear of a kitchen where you can't spill anything?"

He laughed. "No."

"I'm gonna go take a shower," she said.

"Me too."

143

They walked toward the locker rooms, through the shade behind the bleachers. "Look at all these violets," Shana said. "Every year, they just keep coming up."

"Yeah," he said. They were both still huffing and puffing.

"People walk all over them in track shoes and everything, and garbage gets dropped on 'em all the time, and they just keep on," she said.

At the doors of the locker rooms, Shana put her hand up against the sun. "I had a good time running," she said. "Thanks for waiting for me."

She scuffed one foot back and forth on the concrete. "I'm sorry about your sister, Nick. That's a tragedy."

"Yeah," he said. "Thanks."

Under the hot water, Nick said to himself that things were going fast. Sometimes you could wait and wait for an hour to pass, and sometimes you turned around and an hour was already gone. He'd told Shana about Dianne. He hardly ever told anybody about her. He was surprised that he'd told her, but for some reason he didn't feel terrible about it. The Winnie-the-Pooh games were fun to remember. Ridiculous little-kid games. Once when he had to be Roo, Dianne made him take the strengthening medicine that Roo had to take in the book, but she made up her own. She put coffee and Ovaltine and maple syrup together, and then she put in orange juice and some vinegar and mayonnaise. She made him swallow two spoons of it. He didn't tell Shana about that, it was just a little thing.

He washed his hair with some shampoo that somebody had left on the shower floor. He did it with one hand, keeping the bandaged arm out of the shower. While he was rubbing in the lather, he remembered another game Dianne had thought of to play. It was dumping the feathers from a leaking pillow into their parents' bed and then making the bed so they wouldn't know. "Maybe a goose came and took a nap in their bed," she said, and they fell on the floor laughing while they waited for their parents to find out.

Silly kids' games.

It's better not to think about it, he said to himself, and turned off the water.

Shana was waiting outside the locker room door. Her hair was soaking wet and it stuck to her head. "I thought you had to go home," he said. He started across the grass to the street.

"I can wait. Listen, Nick. I thought of something in the shower. It's funny you like frogs so much."

He stopped on the grass and looked at her. Maybe she just didn't want to go home and get yelled at yet.

"I mean, they can breathe in the water, then they can come out and sit on a rock or something, they still stay alive." Some drops of water fell off her hair onto her neck.

"Yeah. That's what makes them amphibians, they evolved that way," he said. He didn't even know why he said it.

"It's too bad people didn't," Shana said, and wiped her neck.

Nick thought of Bruce actually diving into the aquarium in Room 19, being a little tiny person like something in a cartoon, just swimming around underwater, breathing and grinning. It was crazy. He sort of laughed.

"Because if they did, your sister would be alive," Shana said.

He didn't want to think about it. The dream would come back. He couldn't stand having that dream again tonight, not when he was beginning to feel not so jagged. Not when Shana had run with him even if her parents were going to yell again. Not when he'd gone back to school even when he thought he should disappear instead.

He looked down at the grass. Somebody had dropped a bent Pepsi can, and he kicked it at the wall of the gym.

Shana watched the can curve through the air. She said, "Well, it's impossible. But wouldn't it be a good thing?"

He looked at her and then looked away, fast. The first thing he saw was the wall of the gym. A blank wall. He kept his eyes on it. He felt as if he was falling a long way into space, falling up into space and down into space at the same time. He needed something to hold on to. He moved his feet farther apart on the grass. He saw shapes, all crowding together. Squares and diamonds and circles and triangles ran around inside his brain, they were all different colors, all bumping into each other. He stared at the corner of the gym wall, the straight line up and down where the wall stopped and air began. He kept his eyes on the straight up-and-down line of the wall.

"Wouldn't it?" Shana said.

He couldn't think of any words. The shapes in his mind didn't have words. They were like something torn apart and trying to be put together. He kept staring at the corner of the wall. He knew Shana was still standing there, but he had the feeling that even if he shouted she wouldn't be able to hear him. He felt upside down, but his feet were still standing on the grass.

Her voice came from ridiculously far away, like somebody calling across a canyon. "Nick, do you think that's why you like amphibians so much?"

She moved her feet on the grass, and he found some words. "I don't know," he said. They weren't the right words. He said them again.

"Well," she said, "maybe I'm wrong. I've gotta go home. Wish me luck." She turned around and walked away.

Nick didn't even really feel his feet taking steps as he walked across the grass to the sidewalk, turned right, walked three blocks, turned left, walked two blocks, and then went through an empty lot to his street. He walked in the door, sat down on the floor, and put his arms around Patsy's neck. He stood up and took off his pack and put it on the floor and then went upstairs to his room. He looked at the book that was open to the Larch Mountain Sal. He flipped the pages. The Monterey Sal, the Van Dyke's Sal, the Pacific Treefrog, the Burrowing Treefrog, the Western Spadefoot Toad, the Colorado River Toad all went past, with their big eyes and their spread toes.

He looked at the wall where the *Star Wars* poster used to be. He looked at the clothes he'd thrown on the floor. He looked at the legs of his desk that he'd sanded with his dad. He looked at the dog hairs on the blankets of his bed. He looked out the window at the forsythia against the fence. He flipped the amphibian pages again. They all went bouncing past: the Dakota Toad, the Cricket Frog, the Tiger Sal, the California Newt, the Pig Frog.

And then he let himself look at the picture of Dianne. He felt himself pounding on her stomach after she was dead. He could feel exactly how his fists hit her bathing suit and hit it and hit it again. He closed his eyes and tried to squeeze them tight shut, he put his hands against his ears, so he could keep out the squishing sound his fists had made on her.

He took his hands away from his ears, he opened his eyes, and looked back at the amphibians. The Red-legged Frog stared at him from the book. He looked out the window again, and watched the bushes waving in the breeze. The sun made long shadows from the bushes across the lawn.

And as he looked across the lawn, he knew Shana was right. If Dianne was an amphibian she could breathe on the bottom of the swimming pool and she would be alive now. That must by why he liked amphibians so much. That was the truth.

He lay down on his bed and stared at the ceiling. It took millions of years to evolve from gills to lungs. Dianne couldn't go back to gills again.

The ceiling above his bed looked like somebody else's ceiling, in somebody else's room. Maybe he was somebody else. Maybe his parents would come home and say, Hi, Nick, and they'd be talking to somebody who wasn't even their son. He felt as if he'd gone to another country and come back with somebody else's thoughts. Or as if he'd turned inside out for a few seconds and then had his skin put back just a little bit differently. He'd look the same, and everybody would be completely fooled.

Or maybe he'd slid down inside himself and come back out, and he was still Nicholas Swansen.

He heard himself breathing in and out slowly. No dog, no parents, no Shana, no Bruce or Jason or Mr. Norton, no cops, no veterinarian, no doctor, no anybody. Sometimes you just needed to be by yourself. To try to find out what was going on.

All this time, your brain was chasing around, doing these weird things. It was putting frogs and proms and your dead sister and your dog and everything else together in pictures you couldn't understand. Your brain was messing around in there, jumbling things up, shaking your thoughts inside out, just waiting for you to wander in and watch. It was making up stories, and thinking up answers to questions you didn't even ask.

And all this time, every second of every minute of every hour of every day, you looked to everybody else as if you were just going along.

He heard the front door open and close, then his mother's voice called up the stairs. "Hi, Nick. How was your day?"

Was it even a day? Maybe it was just a minute long, maybe it was months. Downstairs was a lady who saw her daughter dead on the white, pebbly edge of somebody's swimming pool nine years ago, and she was asking, How was your day?

"Hi, Mom," he called.

She was humming something, and he heard keys clink onto a table. She put a record on to play. Nick stared at the ceiling.

"Nick," his mother called, "this is Beethoven's last string quartet."

He lifted his left arm and looked at the bandage. He'd kept it mostly out of the shower, but it was wet at the bottom edge, and it was kind of dirty. Beethoven was deaf and he couldn't do math and he wasn't a good dancer.

"You know what he wrote on it?" His mother was calling to him again. "He wrote on a page of it, 'Must it be?' And then he wrote the answer: 'It must be.' He asked that question and then he answered it." His mother stopped talking. The music kept on playing.

Nick watched a fly rubbing two of its legs together on his desk lamp. He heard a clumping sound. Beethoven must have a drum in his string quartet. It got closer. Then Patsy stood in his open doorway, staring at him. She couldn't climb stairs in her heavy splint. But she did. She walked in, lay down beside his bed, and began to lick a paw. Whenever she landed anywhere, her splint made a thud.

Probably Beethoven didn't want something to be, but it was, so he said on the music, "It must be." It was something Beethoven couldn't do anything about.

Listening to the music probably made Nick's mother feel better about things.

He looked at Patsy licking away at her paw.

Probably Shana was sorry for what she did about the prom. But you couldn't really tell with girls.

He reached down and scratched Patsy's head. Probably his brain was crazy for liking amphibians and getting Dianne mixed up with them.

The music was okay. It wasn't like the song about "Stay with me baby I want you to play with me baby tonight," but it was okay.

Probably the bomb wouldn't drop tomorrow, probably his dad would get home in a few minutes and remind him about the driving lesson on Saturday. Probably his mother

would say, "Isn't this music nice?" And his dad would probably say, "Yes. Yes it is. Very."

Probably he was still Nick Swansen.

He rested his hand between Patsy's ears and closed his
eyes.